DATE DUE
REMINDER

OCT 0 3 2000

Please do not remove
this date due slip.

THE TRUTH ABOUT KIM O'HARA

ERIKA TAMAR

Atheneum   1992   New York

Maxwell Macmillan Canada
Toronto

Maxwell Macmillan International
New York   Oxford   Singapore   Sydney

Atheneum
Macmillan Publishing Company
866 Third Avenue
New York, NY 10022

Maxwell Macmillan Canada, Inc.
1200 Eglinton Avenue East
Suite 200
Don Mills, Ontario M3C 3N1

Macmillan Publishing Company is part of the
Maxwell Communication Group of Companies.

First edition
Printed in the United States of America
10 9 8 7 6 5 4 3 2 1

Library of Congress Cataloging-in-Publication Data
Tamar, Erika.
The truth about Kim O'Hara / Erika Tamar.—1st ed.
p.   cm.
Sequel to: It happened at Cecilia's.
Summary: Fifteen-year-old Andy is often baffled by his girlfriend
Kim's apparent coolness and rigidity until her tragic past is
suddenly revealed.
ISBN 0–689–31789–1
[1. Interpersonal relations—Fiction.   2. Emotional problems—
Fiction.   3. Vietnamese Americans—Fiction.   4. New York (N.Y.)—
Fiction.]   I. Title.
PZ7.T159Tv   1992
[Fic]—dc20   92–3943

To the fabulous Bookends

"LORRAINE," I called, "where's my red shirt?"

I couldn't keep Kimberly O'Hara waiting!

"What?" she answered from the living room.

I rummaged through all my dresser drawers. I tried my closet. The hangers were jammed together; I went through all of them.

I checked the hooks way in the back. My skateboard rolled out and smashed into my ankle. Damn, that hurt! Ever since my dad and Lorraine got married last year, all my stuff has been crowded. Don't get me wrong—I liked Lorraine a lot, but it was tough on closet space.

I limped into the living room.

She looked up from the real estate section of last Sunday's *Times*. "Listen to this, Andy. Twelfth Street, off Fifth Avenue. Three bedrooms, three baths, terrace, twenty-four-hour doorman, fifteenth floor. . . . They don't say how much—"

"I'll bet they don't. Have you seen my red shirt?"

"It'll turn up. . . . West Village, historic district, town house with garden, needs TLC. . . ."

"I need it *now!*"

Lorraine looked puzzled. "You need tender loving care?"

"No, my shirt!"

"Why so important?"

"Because I'm meeting *Kim O'Hara!*"

"Kim O'Hara? Isn't she the one who pierced your ear?"

"Right. And I'm meeting her in *ten minutes.*"

"What's she going to do, pierce your other ear?"

"No!"

Lorraine grinned. "Well, that's a relief."

The only thing Dad and Lorraine associated with Kim O'Hara was the ear piercing. Lorraine had been okay about that. She'd tried to calm Dad down. She kept saying a lot of guys wore an earring and he kept slapping his forehead and saying, "*Why? Why?* Did you need *another* hole in your head?"

"You have other shirts," Lorraine said.

She didn't understand. It was a Girbaud and I liked the way it was cut; it made me look muscular. I grabbed a tan shirt—at least it was clean—and I threw on a sweater.

"You look very nice, Andy."

It was too late to think about it.

"Have a good time."

I ran the four blocks to the theater. The Waverly was featuring a series of Marx Brothers comedies. On this particular Saturday night, it was *A Day at the Races*. No one breaks me up the way the Marx Brothers do. I figured we'd laugh a lot—laughing is the sign of a good time, right? breaks the ice, right?—and maybe make out a little, I mean, if she liked me. . . . Then we'd go someplace after, any place she wanted; the Village is full of good spots. I'd been saving up my cash. This was a mega-important Saturday night.

I got there just before she did.

"Hi," I said.

"Hi."

She looked at my ear. "I see you've still got it."

I fingered the gold stud. "Uh-huh."

I hadn't actually had a craving for an earring. I got it because Kim was in my ninth grade French class last year, and I'd been watching her all term. She was half Chinese and half Irish, with huge almond eyes, a little upturned nose, and full, pink lips; that added up to one hundred degrees beyond cute. Kim O'Hara was independent and cool, real cool.

I wasn't shy—back in junior high, they used to call me Andy "the Mouth" Szabo—but she was intimidating. God, I used to be so immature. I used to throw paper airplanes at the back of her head in class; she'd demolish me with a calm lift of her perfect eyebrows. One day, I cornered her at her locker and I couldn't think of anything to say and I kept staring at the little gold earrings dangling from her perfect lobes.

"I'm—uh—thinking of getting my ear pierced," was what I'd finally come up with. "And—uh—did it hurt?"

"I could do it for you," she'd said.

That was about as receptive as she'd ever been—and that's about as far as I got in ninth grade. But then, after school let out for the summer, she'd phoned me. She didn't have anything in particular to do that afternoon and if I still wanted my ear pierced . . . Well, I went booking straight over to her house. It was a mess of ice cubes and blood and silk thread scraping through the wound, but it was worth it. After the bloodletting, we'd walked along Sixth Avenue looking for a gold stud and talked and stuff. But she was leaving for the summer with her parents—Maine or someplace north like that—and I hadn't seen her since.

Anyway, here she was, finally, in person. She had

a bit of a tan left over from the summer. She looked so hot it made my toes curl up.

We stopped at the candy counter. "What do you like?" I said.

"Let's share some popcorn."

"One large popcorn. With lots of butter," I told the attendant. "How about soda and Hershey's bars? And Milk Duds? Anything you want. Cracker Jack? Emeralds?"

She smiled. "Just popcorn. I don't want to get too fat."

Fat! She was mostly skinny—and curvy just where she was supposed to be. I mean, she did one hell of a lot for the fuzzy pink top she was wearing.

"Well—how's your high school?" she asked.

"Oh." I pulled my attention from the fuzzy pink-ness. "It's hard to tell the first week. I think I'll like it. Yours?"

"Very good."

We found center seats in the dark.

"I saw this one a couple of years ago," I told her. "It's funny."

Right from the beginning, the audience got into the spirit of Groucho, Harpo, and Zeppo. But something was very wrong.

It wasn't the film—same hilarious routines, and everybody in the packed house was roaring. Me too, at first, until I realized Kim wasn't even cracking a smile. I was in the middle of a Charles Addams cartoon. Remember the one with a big movie audience weeping except for the monster in the front row who's yukking up a storm? Picture it in reverse, with me and Kim in the center.

"Uh—Kim—you want some popcorn?" I offered the container.

"Okay, thanks." A couple of kernels went into the perfect mouth. The perfect profile remained stony.

I put my arm around the back of her seat. Didn't dare let it drop down around her shoulders.

Groucho paced maniacally and Harpo blew his horn. I kept glancing at her. Nothing. The movie rolled on and on.

"Listen, if you're not in the mood for this . . ." I said.

"It's good," she said.

"If you want to leave—we could do something else—"

"No. Well, not unless *you* want to . . ."

"No. I thought maybe *you* did . . . ," I said.

The guy in front of us turned around and said "Shhh."

So much for conversation.

In the dim light, I could see that she was holding her arms crossed in front of her chest.

"Are you cold?" I said.

"No. Why?"

"Well—I thought—you want my sweater?"

"No thanks."

The guy in front of us said "Shhh."

She was having a rotten time. She hated me. That's what it was—she hated me. Something must have turned her off. I'd taken a shower. I'd brushed my teeth. Maybe I had B.O. and halitosis anyway. And dandruff, ring around the collar . . .

People were rolling in the aisles as Harpo pushed a horse. Kim stared deadpan at the screen. I slouched in my seat.

Maybe it was the cat hairs all over my sweater; my cat, Katie, sheds a lot. I should have found time to brush them off.

The credits trailed to an end and we exited onto Seventh Avenue. It was one of those Indian-summer September nights and everybody was out. Saturday night in the Village means a crowd: bridge-and-tunnel groups, local punks, suburban wannabee punks, college kids, older couples, panhandlers, families. There were still tables out on the sidewalk in front of the cafés. The piano bars were in full swing.

I'd been thinking of taking her over to Maxie's on MacDougal. Maxie knows my dad—most of the restaurant and club owners in the neighborhood know each other—so I'd get VIP treatment there. Maybe the evening could be salvaged.

"We could go to Maxie's," I said. "They've got a good band. The Psychotics."

"Well—I don't know. . . ."

"Or the Carousel or—?"

"No, I'd better not," Kim said. "I can't get home too late."

"Too late? It's not even eleven."

"I really have to get up early tomorrow. I have a lot to do."

Okay, I knew when I was being blown off. Politely but definitely.

"So you want to go home?" I said.

She nodded.

Kim lived in one of those high rises off Fifth Avenue. We walked past Washington Square Park. I was all through trying.

"It's a beautiful night," Kim said.

I was too crushed to answer.

I slunk along next to her.

"I'd love to see *A Night at the Opera*," she said. "I think that's playing next week."

The arch looked mysterious behind shadowy trees.

"Do you want to?" she asked.

"Want to what?"

"See *A Night at the Opera* next week?"

I stopped short. "Wait a minute. You want to see another *Marx Brothers* movie? With *me*? Next week?"

"That's what I just said." She looked down at the ground. "Not if you don't want to. . . ."

Maybe I was finally, irretrievably, cracking up. Maybe I was hallucinating. "You do?"

"It was really fun."

"I thought you hated the whole thing."

"Why would you think that?"

"Kim, you know, you didn't laugh once. Not once."

"Just because I don't laugh out loud—"

"You didn't even smile."

"I don't laugh out loud in movies. I laugh kind of . . . inwardly."

"That's very strange," I said.

"You can't expect everyone to be just like you, Andy. I can have a really great time without bouncing around and making a lot of noise."

"I don't bounce!"

"Oh, you know what I mean. You're so . . . active. That's what I like about you."

"You like something about me?"

She smiled that killer smile. "I like everything about you."

She liked me! That's what she said—she liked me! "But—then why am I taking you right home?"

"I have a lot to do in the morning."

"On *Sunday morning?*"

"There's a test Monday. Physics. Bronx Science is *hard.*"

"You know you'll ace it," I said. She'd been valedictorian at our junior high graduation. "Come on, let's go to Maxie's and—"

"No, I have to work for my As. It doesn't come easy."

"So you'll get an A minus. Let's—"

"You don't understand. I have to get an *A.*"

She sounded so uptight about it. She probably had driving parents, the kind that see a B as a major tragedy. I wasn't exactly looking forward to meeting them.

"THANKS, Andy," Kim said, when we came to the front door of her building. "Well . . . good night."

"Good night. . . ." The sidewalk was quiet and dark. I was about to make my move—I was within the critical five inches—when the doorman popped out and opened the glass doors.

"I'll take you in," I said.

"Okay."

The doorman stayed in the vestibule. So far, so good. We headed for the elevator bank in a dimly lit alcove—and there was a concierge looking at us from behind his desk.

"I'll go upstairs with you," I said.

"All right." She pushed the number twelve button. I hoped it was a very slow elevator.

Just as the doors were sliding shut, an old woman

with a yipping terrier squeezed in with us.

"Now be a good boy, Jonathan," the woman said.

Kim and I studied the tiled floor. The dog yipped all the way up to twelve.

In front of her apartment door, Kim looked up at me and her mouth was a magnet. I kissed her. Her lips parted and her hand brushed the back of my neck. She smelled wonderful—some kind of gardenia perfume. She fit into my arms just right.

"I really have to go in."

I couldn't help kissing her again.

"No, really, good night, Andy." Her eyes reflected the bright hall light.

"I'll call you tomorrow."

"Okay." She smiled. "Good night, Andy."

"Good night. . . ."

I levitated all the way home. I was too psyched to even consider sleep, so I went downstairs to Cecilia's. That's my dad's place—the city's best Hungarian-Cajun restaurant. Well, the city's *only* Hungarian-Cajun restaurant. After dinner hours, the bar crowd hangs out; some of the comics from the club across the street were trying out new routines on each other and playing can-you-top-this. It was terrific, so I didn't go up to bed until late.

I wasn't in a hurry to wake up the next morning— I wanted to doze for a while and think about Kim—

but my cat kept jumping on me. Then the smell of coffee and French toast drew me into the kitchen.

". . . and there's a working fireplace in the bedroom. It just needs to be opened up and cleaned. Lazlo, it's so perfect. . . . Good morning, Andy."

" 'Morning." I poured a cup of coffee and sat down with them.

I'd kissed Kim O'Hara. After all those junior high years . . .

"French toast on the stove," Dad said. "I kept it warm for you."

"I know, that's what got me up." Dad makes it with grated orange peel and it's the best.

". . . and there's still a lot of the old molding and . . . Andy, you know about it."

"About what?"

"The town house. Remember the ad I read to you last night? The one that needs TLC? I went to see it this morning and—"

Lorraine is one of those disgusting morning people. She wakes up early, and cheerful.

"—and it's run down, but it has so much potential."

"I don't know," Dad said. "Renovating can be—"

I remembered just the way Kim's lips felt. I kept smelling gardenias.

Lorraine's voice was bumping into my thoughts;

". . . just *cosmetic* renovation . . . basically in good shape . . . the first place I've really fallen in love with . . ."

I didn't know about falling in *love,* but Kim had said she liked me.

"Just how run-down is it?" Dad asked.

"Years of scaling wallpaper on top of old wallpaper . . . lots of little cubby rooms . . . We'd have to break down some walls to—"

Kisses, I thought, were a lot like eating peanuts. One was never enough.

"Break down *walls?* How many walls?" Dad said.

"Oh, five or six," Lorraine said airily.

"The cost of labor . . . construction costs—"

I went to the stove to help myself to French toast. I couldn't wait to see her again.

"That's just it!" Lorraine said. "We'll do the work ourselves! Put in the sweat equity and wind up with the most beautiful home. Lazlo, there's a little garden in the back. It needs a lot of work, but—"

"I have to be in the restaurant. I won't have that much time—"

"I know. I thought Andy and I—"

I whirled around. "Me?"

"We could do it. You'd work with me, wouldn't you, Andy? We'd get a professional for the plumbing, but—"

"Sounds like it needs more than tender loving care. Sounds like it needs an emergency room," Dad said.

"I'm serious, we could do it. Andy, can I count on you?"

I sat down. "Sure, I'll break walls with you. Sort of like demolition derby."

"Lorraine, wait, what do we know about construction?" Dad said. "Chicken *paprikás,* fine. Walls, no."

"We can learn!" Lorraine said. "I mean, every single hard hat isn't necessarily a mental giant."

"I'm sorry, hon," Dad said, "I don't think—"

"Will you guys at least look at it? Keep an open mind and look at it?" Lorraine seemed like the fluffy poodle type, but like a pit bull, she held on to things. She was like that about her dancing too—went to class every single day, danced her heart out in all the off-Broadway flops she'd been in.

"I'll *look* at it," Dad said, "but—"

"Tomorrow?" Lorraine said. Cecilia's is closed on Mondays.

"Okay, okay," Dad said.

"How large is this house?" I got the words out around a big mouthful.

"Well," Lorraine said, "it's *high*. Four stories. It's—uh—very thin, so it would be like one large room to a floor."

"You mean my room on my own floor? All to myself?"

"Yes. I thought you'd probably take the top floor."

"I like it," I said.

"There's the cutest spiral staircase—"

"A *thin* house?" Dad said.

"It's no more than a couple of blocks from Cecilia's, so it's perfect, Lazlo."

Dad laughed. "A perfect wreck."

After a while, Dad went downstairs to take care of the lunch crowd and Lorraine got lost in the Sunday *Times*. I flipped through the sports section and couldn't keep my mind on what I was reading.

I went to the telephone. It has a very long cord, and I pulled it into the bathroom for privacy. Dad calls the bathroom my phone booth.

"Hello," Kim said.

"Hi. It's Andy."

"Oh, hi!" I swear, she sounded enthusiastic.

"What are you doing?"

"Still studying."

"How about taking a break?"

"I don't know. . . ."

"A short break? Come on, Kim."

"Well, a very short one. . . . You could quiz me."

"I'll be right over!"

"Andy, bring some homework or something.

Maybe we could study together."

Homework was not exactly what was on my mind. "I guess—I have some reading to do for American lit."

"What are you reading?"

"*Zen and the Art of Motorcycle Maintenance.*"

"Really? We have Stephen Crane and Nathaniel Hawthorne."

"My high school is very Zen," I said.

"What do you mean?"

"I'll tell you about it. I'll be right over."

I rushed into my room to get dressed. "I still can't find my red shirt!"

Nothing from Lorraine. At least she didn't say things like "look where you left it." My friend Garrity's mother is full of zingers. That, and "if it was up your nose, you'd know where it was."

I looked through my closet again. This time, I kept one foot pushing back the skateboard. "It has to be somewhere!"

"Are you going out?" Lorraine called. "I thought maybe you'd look at the town house this afternoon."

"I'll see it with Dad tomorrow."

Not that I wasn't interested. We needed to move someplace bigger. But right then my only thought was of being near Kim as fast as I could get there.

"FORCE equals what?" I mumbled, stifling a yawn. We had been at it for more than an hour.

"Mass times acceleration."

Kim's living room was airy and bright. The sunshine streaming in made the oranges and reds of the Persian rug glow.

"Andy? Is that right?"

"You know it's right. You didn't get one wrong yet." I tried moving closer to her on the couch. It was soft and squashy, the kind you sink into. I couldn't make the subtle move I'd intended. I wound up lunging across to get my arm around her shoulder. She laughed.

"What's funny?" Her face was close to mine. She had the longest eyelashes.

"That was major acceleration," she said. "A body

at rest tends to stay at rest and a body in motion—"

"Speaking of bodies"—I put my other arm around her and she snuggled against me—"and magnetic attraction . . ."

"In a magnetic force field—," she started, and I covered her lips with mine. Her lips were full and soft.

One kiss blurred into another. We sank into the cushions. *Basic Physics* hit the carpet with a soft thud.

I could feel her bra hook through the silky thing she was wearing. I wanted to bring my hand around to the front, to the full curves pressing against my chest. No, better not. Not yet. Lightning ricocheted along my spine and I didn't want to come up for air. The heat was rising—well, that wasn't all that was rising. . . .

She twisted away. "Andy—"

"Don't stop," I whispered.

"My folks. I hear the key."

I sat up straight so fast it made me dizzy. I adjusted my shirt. Kim was running her fingers through her hair, neatening it. There was a giveaway redness around her lips.

"Should I go?" I said, panicked.

"Of course not. I want my parents to meet you."

God, I couldn't meet them *now*! My shirt—maybe I could pull it out to cover—if it was long enough . . .

Too late. They were in the room. "Mom and Dad, this is Andy Szabo. And this is my sister, Tracey."

I jumped to my feet to shake hands. I prayed they wouldn't notice the bulge. It was out of control. I crossed one leg over the other and forced myself to concentrate on optimum politeness.

"How do you do, Mr. and Mrs. O'Hara." My voice came out high and slightly hysterical. "Tracey." I was strangling.

Mr. O'Hara was a big guy with a firm grip. "Well, Andy, glad to meet you." He gave me an encouraging smile.

I quickly stuck my hand deep in my jeans pocket. Maybe they would take it for an oversized hand.

Tracey was staring at me. I stared back. She was about twelve, with a face full of freckles.

"Please, sit down." Mrs. O'Hara had freckles too, under a dusting of powder. Her eyes were blue and friendly behind dark-rimmed glasses.

I sank down and surreptitiously placed a small sofa pillow on my lap. Pure stress seemed to be taking care of my problem.

"Kimmie, you missed a fun time, but we brought something home for you." Mrs. O'Hara emptied a small paper bag and put some pastry on napkins on the coffee table. "Dig in, kids."

"We went to that Ninth Avenue street fair—you know, wall-to-wall ethnic food," Mr. O'Hara said.

"It was awfully crowded," Kim's mom said. Wait a minute . . . Kim's mom? I'd thought she'd be Chinese. Kim must have been adopted.

"Boy, did we pig out!" Tracey said.

"Help yourself, Andy," Mr. O'Hara said. "Kourambiedes."

I clutched the pillow. What? What was he saying? I glanced at Kim. She was looking at her dad, cool and collected, no help at all.

"Greek cookies," Tracey said.

"Oh. Love them," I said. "Thanks."

I took a crumbly bite. There was a rim of powdered sugar around Tracey's lips. She was still staring at me. Kim wasn't eating; she gave me a little smile.

I was making a terrible first impression, I knew it. I was going straight downhill.

"How about some Coke or apple cider?" Mrs. O'Hara said.

"Apple cider. Oh. No thanks," I said.

Mr. O'Hara filled the awkward pause. "Well . . . do you go to Bronx Science too?"

"No, sir. I go to Bayard-Trent."

"Bayard-Trent . . . sounds familiar. . . ."

"It's in the Village, sir. It's a very small school, sir."

"Private school, right?"

"Yes, sir."

"Do you like it?" Mr. O'Hara asked.

"Yes, sir, so far." Too many *sirs* were pouring out of my mouth. I took a breath and forced myself into normal-conversation mode. "I wanted to go there because they have a lot of writing—screen-writing and journalism and stuff—and there's a good school newspaper and magazine."

"Andy worked on the newspaper in junior high," Kim said. "He wrote some wonderful articles."

I didn't know she'd read them. I didn't know she'd noticed me at all. I could feel a big, dumb grin breaking out all over my face.

Mr. O'Hara sighed. "Seems to me the schools now work you kids too hard," he said. "It's not right to be home studying on a beautiful day like this."

"Oh, I agree with you," I said. He seemed okay. I looked at Kim. "Maybe we could take a break? Go out for a walk or something?"

"Good idea," Mrs. O'Hara said. "Poor Kimmie's been cooped up all day."

*   *   *

We walked down Fifth Avenue holding hands. Her hand was small and delicate next to mine.

"They're very nice," I said.

"Mmm-hmm."

"I thought your parents would be . . . sort of strict . . . and formal."

She looked at me, puzzled. "No, they're not strict at all. Well, we have some rules, but they make sense."

"Like what?"

"Like I have to tell them where I'm going, and I have to call if I'm going to be late. I don't have any problem with that."

"No, I guess not. . . . And I thought your mother would be Chinese. You're part Chinese, aren't you?"

"Why would you think that? Do you think all Asians are Chinese?"

"What? No. I guess I just always thought—"

"That's as stupid as if I decided all North Americans were . . . were New Yorkers."

"It's a natural mistake, Kim." We lived close to Chinatown and a lot of the kids in the junior high were—

"It's not natural, it's stupid!"

"Are we having our first fight?" I said. " 'Cause if we are, I don't know what it's about."

"I'm Vietnamese," she said. "Half Vietnamese.

Listen, there are probably as many different kinds of Asians as —it's just plain ignorant not to know anything about the geography and history and culture of most of the world's population and—"

"Okay, you're right." She looked cute when she got wound up. "So you'll teach me all about Vietnamese culture."

She shrugged. "I don't know all that much about it. . . . Anyway, you've seen my mom before."

"When?"

"Last year. When we had dinner at your dad's restaurant."

"Oh, right. I was bussing that night."

"You dropped a tray."

"I didn't get much of a look at your parents. It was pretty dark, and anyway, I was busy staring at you."

"You were?"

"That's why I dropped the tray."

We had come to Washington Square Park. There were women with baby carriages, college kids kicking a soccer ball around, and some street people on the fringes. We looked for an empty bench. A raggedy guy was sprawled out full length on one of the benches.

"The police should get rid of them," she muttered.

"He's not bothering anybody." He had a pile of

newspapers for a pillow. His arm was over his eyes. "Being homeless has to be the worst."

"The grass in the park used to be nice before *they* started hanging out," Kim said. "Anyway, I love this time of day. Just before the sun sets, when it's low in the sky."

"It's nice," I agreed.

We sat down on a bench at the west end.

"A little later on is the hour the French call *l'heure bleu*. We went to Paris two summers ago. It didn't look blue to me, but it sounds romantic, doesn't it?"

"I'm one hundred percent for romance," I said. "Totally. I believe in it. Absolutely."

"My parents liked you."

"They think I'm an idiot."

"No, they liked you. I could tell."

"I hope so. I'm planning to—to be around a lot. . . . Your mom calls you Kimmie."

"It's one of those silly pet names."

I twirled one little strand of her hair around my finger. The rest was perfectly scissored, shining jet. "Can I call you Kimmie?"

"Only if you absolutely have to."

"Okay, Kimmie. So, they adopted you?"

"Well, partly."

"What do you mean, partly? Do you mind my

asking, like personal stuff? I want to know everything." I touched the edge of her collar.

"I don't mind." Her fingernail traced the outline of my hand. "This feels like the start of something."

The way she looked at me made me feel ten feet tall.

"Okay, here's my story," she said. "My dad's my real father. And my mom adopted me."

"That's kind of like me," I said. "My dad's my real father and Lorraine's my stepmother. They got married last year."

"No, that's different," she said. "You were there from the beginning."

The way she said that, kind of sad and wistful, gave me a funny feeling. "You weren't?"

"No, I was five. They were already a family before I came."

"Kim . . . is everything cool between you and your folks? Your Mom?"

"Oh sure. They're the best. I'm just saying it's different from you, but it's fine. I think I'm so lucky, especially when I see some other kids' parents."

"I know what you mean. How did you—I mean, why—?"

"It's a nice story. A love story," she said. "Dad was attached to information services in Saigon, you know, during the war, and my birth mother was an interpreter. She spoke fluent French and English, and Vietnamese, of course, and a smattering of other— anyway, they fell in love. It was *love*, not one of those wartime things. She was pregnant with me and they would have gotten married, but then Saigon fell and he couldn't get her out. He tried everything, but— She died when I was three and—well, he tried to come for me, but they wouldn't let him in until much later."

She spoke quickly, rattling it off like something well-memorized.

"He looked and looked for me. He'd married Mom by then, and after Tracey was born he kept thinking he really had *two* daughters. He says it was like looking for a needle in a haystack, but he never gave up, and finally he found me. You know, my birth mother named me Kimberly because she thought that sounded American and she hoped that I'd live in America one day; that's what she wanted for me. So now here we are, with a happy ending." She finished with a big, bright smile.

I had about a million questions. I held them back. Her smile was too big and bright.

I went to see the town house with Dad and Lorraine on Monday afternoon.

It was tall and thin, just the way Lorraine had described it. We stood on the sidewalk and stared.

"I really don't think—" Dad finally said. "Lorraine, that's—uh—a *very* thin house."

"Please, wait till you see the inside," she pleaded. "The rooms go all the way back; they widen a bit and—Lazlo, it's a steal. There's so much charm; look at that gate. No one does that kind of handwork anymore."

The low wrought-iron gate was intricate with loads of curlicues. It enclosed the small area in front of the stoop.

"Imagine pots of geraniums alongside . . ." Lorraine said.

There was an old-fashioned lantern with more curlicues at the front door. The door creaked as Lorraine
opened it with the real estate agent's key. She patted
it. "Solid oak."

The first level was broken up into three tiny rooms
by two walls. It widened toward the back, giving the
whole thing a strange triangular shape. The floor was
covered by cracked, dark green linoleum. The air was
stale and musty.

"After the walls are torn down, there'd be an open
dining room–kitchen, and look at that beautiful back
window. Look at that garden view. With lots of white
paint and light streaming in from the back and front
windows . . ." Lorraine bent down and peeled off a
piece of loose linoleum. "Look. Herringbone par-
quet!"

Dad examined it. "That's beautiful quality under
all the dirt. If it's not damaged underneath . . . If it
were scraped . . ."

"We could rent a floor scraper for a couple of
days," she said quickly, "and then a few coatings of
polyurethane . . ."

I couldn't believe they were serious. At first
glance, it was shabby and extremely peculiar. But as
Lorraine continued the tour, I almost began to see it
through her eyes.

Second floor. "Only one wall to take out and here's

our living room. That's a marble fireplace; all it needs is cleaning. And there's another working fireplace in our bedroom! Look at that carved molding. After we remove the wallpaper . . ."

I wondered about the demented mind that had chosen the faded wallpapers. They got progressively worse. By the third floor—"Our bedroom, Lazlo"— it had degenerated into gigantic purple grapes and overripe bananas.

"The bathroom is all Portuguese tile. After it's polished, it would be—"

"Nice, but the toilet is missing," Dad said.

Lorraine led the way through the narrow hall. "Do you mind taking the fourth floor, Andy? I know it's a steep climb, but I've always wanted a fireplace in my bedroom; yours doesn't have one, but it's the largest room, plenty of room for a desk and . . ."

We followed her up the spiral staircase and there it was. The first three floors went up kind of straight, but the top floor bulged out like an onion dome. My room was *round*, bisected by a wall with a big arched doorway. Fantastic! I could have this round room all by itself on its own private floor; and with the wall in the middle knocked down, there'd be windows all around. The wallpaper was the worst yet—mustard-colored monkeys swinging from lime green trees— but there was a view of the Village rooftops and the

Jefferson Market library and you could even see the Empire State Building in the distance.

"Can I have a round bed?" I asked.

"We don't know if the house is structurally sound," Dad said.

"The agent is positive that it is," Lorraine said. "Of course, we'd have an engineer inspect it first, but—"

"It probably is a steal," Dad said, "but the only way we could swing it is if we really do most of the work ourselves."

"It would be an adventure," Lorraine said.

"I have to think." Dad was walking around knocking on the walls. I don't know what he was listening for.

I followed him. "Can I have a round bed?"

"Possibly," Dad said. "Andy, if we're even going to consider this, you'd have to commit to pitching in."

At night, with the city lights glittering through all those windows, my room would be a seduction special, for sure; and of course, I imagined Kim in that possibly round bed. I'd paint the room black, have black satin sheets, the works.

"I want it!" I said. "I'll definitely help. I'll scrape the wallpaper off every wall in the house. My project, I promise!"

When I looked closely, I swear I saw some of the monkeys indulging in X-rated activities.

*　　*　　*

Kim and I were going out, but our activities weren't X-rated. They weren't even PG. Before I knew her, when I used to admire her from afar in junior high, I'd thought she was cool and sophisticated and probably hung out with older guys. After a few weeks with her, I'd come to realize her cool was mostly reserve, and she had hardly dated at all.

I went out with Lizabeth Campbell back in eighth grade for like a month, but mostly because we were in the same crowd and were kind of thrown together. It was different with Kim; we were older now and we really liked each other. She was the prettiest girl that had ever liked me back.

The way the guys talk, when you're seriously going out with someone, you're supposed to get it on or at least close to it. Okay, Kim was reserved; maybe she needed more time. She seemed to like kissing me, but that was absolutely all. I took a lot of cold showers; I found out cold showers don't solve a thing. I must be a glutton for exquisite torture; I wanted to be with her all the time. But on weekday nights, there was always something. She had a test coming up or a report or she had to study.

"No one's *that* busy," I exploded on the phone

one day. "If you don't want to see me, just say so."

"I want to see you. Do you think I like working so hard?"

"Then don't."

"I have to. Bronx Science is *tough*. The place is *full* of junior high valedictorians. I have to scramble just to keep up."

"Oh, come on. So settle for a B plus once in a while."

"I can't do that."

"Mike Pello goes to Science too, and I see him hanging out all the time."

"Well, that's Mike Pello. Maybe he's smarter than me."

"Why do you have to be the best?" I heard her exasperated sigh. "No, wait, I'm not arguing, I'm really asking. Do you like science that much? Not the school, the subject."

"Bio's okay. Physics is kind of boring."

"I mean, do you want to be a doctor or some kind of scientist? Is it like a lifelong ambition?" I could relate to that.

"No, not really. Maybe I'd like to be a doctor. . . . I might want to go to law school. Or work in some big corporation. I don't know. I want to go to Harvard or Yale or one of those and—and be very successful."

"The goal is just *success?*"

"There's nothing wrong with that," she said. "What's wrong with success?"

"Nothing," I said. Aha, I thought. My theory was that it had something to do with being adopted. Maybe she had to keep proving herself so her parents would never be sorry. That was almost classic. But Mr. O'Hara was her real father, and Mrs. O'Hara seemed very warm and loving.

Maybe Kim needed *more* love—from me. "Well, how about this afternoon? For a little while?"

"I have to do piano practice."

"Hey, that's great! I didn't know you played the piano!"

"My lesson's tomorrow."

That's what's so terrific when you first start going out—discovering all those new things about someone. "I want to come and listen, okay?"

"Well . . ."

"I swear, I'll listen and not say a word. I won't bother you."

"Well, okay. But I'm really going to practice. For an hour."

"Okay," I said. "No problem. What are you working on?"

" 'Clair de lune,' " she said.

"I'll be right over."

I couldn't wait to hear her. I wasn't a classical music buff, but I was willing to learn. Anyway, "Clair de lune" would be easy listening; good thing it wasn't Wagner. "Clair de lune"—light of the moon. I could picture her in moonlight, moonlight shining on her hair, smiling a mysterious, sensitive smile as melting notes flowed out of her fingers on the moonlit ivories. Yeah, I knew it was the middle of the afternoon, but what's wrong with the romantic view?

It wasn't anything like that.

Her face was grim. And "Clair de lune" was being butchered.

Look, I never pretended I was some kind of musical expert—I took saxophone in third grade and that lasted for about three and a half weeks—but even I could tell. Kim wasn't what you would call musical. I could understand hitting some clinkers when you were just learning a piece, but she was hammering exactly the right notes, grimly and mechanically, and making it come out like a march.

It was painful. It was embarrassing.

I'd promised I wouldn't bother her, so I made myself sit there, quietly, until her hour was up. She sure wasn't enjoying it. She kept on right down to the wire. I'd never seen a kid with that much self-discipline. Hell, I'd never seen a grown-up like that either. It was scary.

When she finished, I didn't know what to say.

"Uh—how long have you been playing?"

"Oh, five years, I guess."

"Five years?"

"I'm not very good yet," she said. "I need a lot more practice."

"Do you like music a lot?" I said.

She shrugged. "Not that much."

"Uh—Kim—are your parents making you take lessons?"

She looked startled. "No. Of course not."

"Then why"—I said it gently—"why do you work so hard at things you don't even like?"

"Because . . ." She hesitated for a moment and whispered, "because I want to be wonderful."

DAD and Lorraine bought the house. There was an inspection and a lot of excitement and a quick closing. I wasn't in on all the details because I was busy adjusting to my new school. Maybe *adjusting* isn't quite the word; going to Bayard-Trent was more like sinking into a tub of warm water. The staff was eagerly solicitous, in line with the brochure's "supportive environment" and "one democratic family with respect for the expression of individual differences." I'd come from a big public junior high and I was taken aback by all that support. During the first week of school, the early hour had been jarring—I'd had a summer of working in Cecilia's at night and sleeping late in the A.M.—and my biological clock was off kilter. I guess I was walking down the hall with a major frown one morning.

A teacher stopped me in the hall. "Is anything wrong, Andy?"

"No." I was startled. "Everything's fine."

"You looked a bit . . . troubled."

"No, just sleepy. Trying not to nod off."

"Sleepy? Nod off? Andy, if there's any problem with—uh—substance abuse, Howie could help—" Howie was Dr. Dindonner, the school psychologist.

"No, I'm fine! Nothing like that, I swear! I'm up too early, that's all."

It's such a small school, it's kind of surprising that they'd have a full-time psychologist. But Bayard-Trent was very into everyone's emotional well-being; so there Dr. Howard Dindonner sat every day, waiting hopefully for someone to come into his office. Occasionally, they let him speak at assemblies. "Coping with Peer Pressure." The real pressure at BT was to prove you're a rugged individualist. "Coping with Fear of Failure." "Coping with Fear of Success." Dr. Dindonner was very big on coping.

"I swear, I don't need to see Dr. Din—"

"All right, if you're sure. . . ." She seemed somewhat disappointed. "I'm Betsy. If you need anything, don't hesitate . . ."

I had to get used to calling teachers by their first names. I had Betsy for history, Ray for biology, Muffy for math.

A girl with flaming red hair was watching the scene. When Betsy left, she said, "Listen kid, if you want to be left alone, you've got to look happy. They'll make us sail trouble-free through troubled adolescence, even if it kills us." She gave me a big phony smile. "Check out my rigor mortis grin."

I laughed. "I'm Andy Szabo."

"I know, you're new. I'll clue you in on this place. I came from the BT lower school, you know, the building on Seventh? I can tell you everything about everybody. First, me. I'm the school rebel."

"You?" She was wearing an alligator polo with chinos, the most conservative kid around; that morning, I'd seen a parade of dashikis, cat suits, motorcycle garb, bustiers. . . .

"Right, me, 'cause I got exhausted from expressing myself. . . . So, do you have a girlfriend?"

"What? Well, yes, I—"

"Oh, snap! You're cute." She laughed at my confusion. "My shrink wants me to work on being more assertive. How'm I doing?"

"You're doing great." She was strange but likable; anyone who thinks I'm cute can't be all bad. "What's your name?"

"P. J. Farroday, but that stinks; call me The Redhead. Got to go. See you. . . ."

I did see her, all the time; she was in every one

of my classes. That wasn't much of a coincidence; almost everyone in tenth grade was in most of my classes. ". . . small groups . . . dedication to personal attention . . ." There were only about twenty people per grade. That was another thing to get used to. You couldn't have any secrets; the school was kind of inbred. The plus side was that I got to know everyone right away. We all hung out together; there weren't enough kids to form cliques. Smallness can remove you from harsh reality. In junior high, my friend Jo-Jo was a great soccer player and I was an also-ran; but BT's team was so limited that I was suddenly thrust into stardom. It was a heady feeling, even on a losing team. It was easy to get into things. The newspaper staff welcomed me with open arms.

The newspaper had won awards and that was one of the reasons I chose BT. BT—that's what everyone called Bayard-Trent. It took a while before I could stop thinking of bacon-and-tomato.

New York City has some terrific public high schools. There's Bronx High School of Science, where Kim goes, and Stuyvesant; they both emphasize science and math, which aren't my areas, and they're awfully hard to get into. Then there's LaGuardia, for music, art, and performance—my friend from junior high, Garrity, goes there. He's a good artist; they took one look at his portfolio and he was in right away. I wasn't sure where I'd fit.

Cecilia's did great business last year—we got a restaurant review in the *Times*—so Dad said I could look into private high schools if I wanted to. A lot of private schools have dress codes. I couldn't see myself in a suit and tie every day; that would totally inhibit my persona. Jo-Jo got a scholarship to Pringley and his dad made him go; he'd have to cope with a *uniform*. I'd heard that BT was kind of free-spirited, and one of their entrance criteria was a writing sample, so here I was. I wasn't sorry. BT was a little weirder than I'd expected, but Mark was an excellent teacher for short story.

The sad thing about high school is that it broke up the old junior high gang. Weeks went by before I could get together with even Jo-Jo and Garrity. Finally we arranged to meet one night at Dominic's Pizzeria on MacDougal. Garrity and I came early and took a booth. We were talking and I saw the tall black kid coming through the door; at first he didn't register as Jo-Jo, then I did a double take.

"Holy cow, what happened to you?" His rasta locks were completely cut off! He looked pathetic.

"You're almost bald!" Garrity exclaimed.

"Had to do it," Jo-Jo mumbled as he slid into the seat. "Pringley."

We shook our heads.

"You know what you look like?" Garrity said. "You look like a preppy!"

"Come on, cut it out. Pringley's okay."

"Look what they did to you! They ruined you!" Garrity said.

"I'm telling you, it's okay. The soccer team's the best, and everybody gets their own computer, and anyway, it's no artsy-fartsy school."

"Man, you haven't seen the girls at LaGuardia," Garrity said. "Some of those dancers are *hot*!"

Jo-Jo grinned. "So how the hell are you guys?" We slapped hands on the tabletop. "Let's have anchovy pizza."

"Okay."

"So, what's happening? Any hot chicks at Bayard-Trent?"

"Some. There's The Redhead, but"—I dropped my bombshell—"I'm going out with an amazing girl. Almost a month now."

"Somebody from Bayard-Trent?"

"No. Someone you know."

"Who?"

I paused for drama. I felt proud; everyone knew she'd been the prettiest girl in junior high. Probably the prettiest anywhere.

"Come on, who?"

"Kim O'Hara," I said, mustering nonchalance.

I glanced from Jo-Jo to Garrity. They looked underwhelmed.

"*Her?*" Garrity said. "The Ice Queen?"

"The what? What did you say?" I was getting mad.

"Watch it, she's his girlfriend," Jo-Jo said, "and Szabo has a short fuse."

"Yeah, sorry," Garrity mumbled.

"But that's what everyone called her," Jo-Jo said.

"I never heard that," I said.

Garrity shrugged.

"She's beautiful," I said. "Well, you know that."

"Yeah," Jo-Jo said. "Mmmm-hmmm."

"And she's sweet. Kind of reserved, but sweet," I said.

"Listen, if you like her, that's all that counts," Garrity said.

I couldn't stand any more. "Okay, what have you guys got against her?"

"Nothing," Jo-Jo said. "I hardly knew her. No one knew her that well. She was standoffish. Kind of prissy."

"Icy," Garrity said. "Uptight all the time. . . . She's beautiful, I'll give you that, but . . ."

I tried not to show hurt. "She's nothing like that," I said. "She's fun when you get to know her."

"If you two get along, hey, that's great," Garrity said.

"Yeah, she probably warms up when she knows

you," Jo-Jo said. "Some girls need time to blossom, that's all. Didn't mean to dis her."

The pizza came and Jo-Jo started talking about Pringley soccer and then we were laughing about all the things we did in junior high. "Hey, remember that big food fight . . . " It was good to hang with them again, but what they'd said about Kim still rankled.

Maybe Jo-Jo was right: Some girls need time to blossom. The Redhead seemed to be in full bloom. The truth is, girls confused me. I mean, I couldn't get the rules straight. When I tried to be a gentleman, like Dad taught me, it could backfire. I was leaving school with The Redhead one day and I went out of my way to open the front door and hold it for her.

"That's a very male chauvinist thing to do. Don't you think I'm capable of opening a door for myself?" she said.

"Oh," I said. "Sorry."

So one night when Kim and I went to the Union Square Cafe, I let her deal with the door. She looked at me like I was a total clod.

"Oh," I said. "Sorry."

The sex thing confused me even more. I had a feeling The Redhead would be enthusiastically responsive. The thought that I'd picked the wrong girlfriend popped into my mind; I squelched it immediately, it was too disloyal. Kim was the one I liked, but . . .

We were alone in her apartment one afternoon. We were in a clinch on the couch and I couldn't get enough of her. Kim was wearing a silky blouse with a line of tiny buttons marching down the front. I could feel her melting against me and I couldn't keep my mind off those buttons. My hand took on a life of its own—one button, two button, three button, four . . . Suddenly she pulled herself out of the mood and shoved me away. "Stop it! I told you *no*! If that's all you're after—"

"No, that's not all I'm after!" I was insulted; I wasn't some animal.

"Well, then stop!"

I was a man dying of thirst on the desert and she was a tall, cool glass of water. I reached for her again. "Come on, Kim, I—"

"I mean it!"

I groaned. "Come on, Kim, there's nothing wrong with—"

"It's wrong for me."

"I'm your *boyfriend*." I tickled the back of her neck. "You like it as much as I do, I can tell."

"No, I don't!" She moved away from me violently. "I do not! It's not right. There's a difference between right and wrong."

"You know something, you've got more stupid rules! Don't you ever do something because you *want* to?"

She jumped up from the couch. "I'll tell you what I don't want! I don't want to be a slut and I don't want to be a hooker!"

"What?" I was stunned. "Who said anything about being a hooker? What're you talking about? Where did that come from?"

"I don't want to talk about it anymore." She wouldn't look at me.

"Kim?"

She shook her head.

It wasn't like I was demanding that she go all the way. Not that I didn't daydream about it, but all I was talking about was a little more. That was normal, I thought. All my friends would be laughing themselves sick if they knew about this scene.

I didn't say anything; she seemed too upset. I thought her reaction was off the wall, but I felt guilty anyway.

She pushed her hair back. "Let's do something else. Let's take a walk."

The last thing I wanted was to do something else, but I said, "Okay, I'll show you my new house."

We held hands on the way; her attack of craziness

had receded. On Waverly Place, I brought her hand up to my lips and she smiled.

"I don't know why we argue so much." She had that certain way of looking at me. "You're my favorite person, Andy."

I really liked her; I'd be more patient and someday, in the right setting—and I had the exact setting in mind—we'd be dynamite together.

"Here it is." I opened the door to my room with a flourish. "Well, what do you think? Great, huh?"

The closed look on her face made me become hyper.

"Check out the windows! Leaded glass! And Lorraine thinks there could be something great under the wallpaper, like old wood with carvings and stuff. Check out the floor! That's herringbone under the dirt!" I sounded like some demented salesman.

"It's . . . different," Kim said.

"It's round!"

"Round?"

"The wall in the middle is coming down and—"

"Oh. Yes," she agreed, "it definitely is round."

"Hey, isn't it great?" Come on, Kim, like it. "And"—I took her hand—"at night, there'll be the city lights, very romantic and . . . it's very, *very* private."

"Why do you need so much privacy?" she said.

"For us."

She gave me a level look.

"Well, we could use a little more—," I started.

"I think we have all the privacy we need."

"You know something? You could at least *pretend* to like it. Just to be polite."

Kim took a quick breath. "It's very unusual."

"You have no imagination. None at all."

"I happen to like things that are brand-new and clean."

"And plastic. Miss Plastic."

"What are you getting so mad about?"

" 'It's very unusual,' " I mimicked. Sheer frustration was turning me into a monster.

She walked away from me toward the window. I looked at her back. Her shoulder blades showed through her blouse.

"I hate it when you're mean," she said in a little-girl voice.

"I'm not mean," I said to her back.

"Yes, you are."

"I thought, when we finally do get to see each other, you'd want a place where we can be alone and—"

"I told you. I'm not going to do anything."

"We could at least get past first base. There's nothing wrong with that," I said to her back.

"You always get right back to the same thing. That's all you ever think about. I don't want to."

"Why not? Why do you always have to be so damn controlled?"

"Well, someone has to be." The light from the window made a halo of her hair.

"I can't turn on and off like a faucet," I said. "It's making me crazy. It's not normal. You're so—so *prissy*!" Jo-Jo's word. It hung in the air between us.

"If you want to break up, go ahead and do it," she finally said.

I wanted to see her face. She wouldn't turn around. Something about her shoulder blades was getting to me.

"Do you?" I mumbled.

Nothing.

"You're not even acting like a girlfriend and . . . " I let my voice trail off. I couldn't tell if she was listening. Her attention was focused out the window.

"Andy?"

"What?"

"There's something going on out there. Come and look."

I went to the window. I wanted to touch her shoulders, but I held back.

"Andy, look."

There was a big crowd of people on the sidewalk in front of the house.

"Something must have happened," I said.

I was looking for some sign of commotion. They seemed perfectly calm, but there were at least twenty people.

"What in the world is that?" she said.

They were all staring up at the windows. They were definitely staring at our windows.

"I don't know," I said.

A man was pointing at the house; he was talking a mile a minute. Some of the people moved closer for a better view.

"What are they—," I started. And then, I realized. "Oh, no!"

"I know what it is!" Kim said simultaneously. "Your house is on a walking tour!"

"My house, on the Village historical landmark tour!"

"So much for your privacy," she said, and we collapsed, laughing, in each other's arms. There were tears in her eyes; I hoped they were from laughing so hard.

Outside, the group drifted over a few feet and was examining the front door. A woman was taking notes.

"This is so funny!"

"I don't believe this. Lorraine will love it."

Long after the group had moved away we were still holding each other.

"I don't want to break up," she said.

"Neither do I."

"Stop pressuring me, though," she said.

"I'm not pressuring you."

"You are. You really are. A lot."

"Okay, I won't," I said. She made me feel like some kind of brute. Hey, I'm a good guy; I'm not insensitive. "I'll try," I said. "But it isn't easy."

IT was one of those bright, crisp Saturday mornings when the streets seem newly cleaned and fresh. Even the air smelled good. On certain autumn days, New York City is the very best place in the world to be.

Kim and I had nothing in particular to do. We were just walking around, no big deal, but I had my arm around her waist and she had her arm around mine, with her thumb in the belt loop of my jeans. Just walking like that, as close as we could get, gave me a great natural high and I could tell she was feeling that way too. Whatever, I swore to myself I wouldn't mention sex today. I wouldn't even let it cross my mind. Which was a lot like trying not to think of a blue elephant.

Sixth Avenue was crowded, with vendors taking up most of the sidewalk. We strolled along, looking at T-shirts and African carvings, but mostly we only had eyes for each other. Her stride matched mine exactly; she was almost as tall as me. You'd expect someone so fine-boned and delicate to be petite; I could easily encircle her wrist with two fingers.

When we passed Urban Outfitters, Kim tugged at my belt loop. "Let's go in, I love this place." I don't know why girls like stores so much, but I was game. I stopped to look at the front wall. It was rough plaster, with dozens of broken dishes and shards of pottery imbedded in it. There was even part of a cup, with the handle sticking out. It was all different colors and patterns.

"That's so cool," I said. "I bet I could do that with my wall." But I'd have to break a hell of a lot of our dishes, I thought; Lorraine would have a fit.

Kim pulled me to the back, where they have hats piled up and spilling over the shelves.

I put a black felt number on her head and pulled it down past her forehead; it had big red roses in the center. "No kidding, it looks great on you."

"Too funky." She grabbed a green velvet beret and posed in it.

"You're beautiful. You'd look beautiful in anything," I said.

"Andy, this one's for you!"

"No, come on." I ducked, but she got the checked cap on my head anyway.

"That's sharp. You ought to get it," she said.

"Naw, I never wear hats."

"No, I guess not. Your hair's so nice, you shouldn't cover it."

"My hair's nice?"

"I always loved your hair," she said. "It's so thick and—I used to look at you in French and I thought you were *so* handsome and smart too. . . ."

I liked being a member of this mutual admiration society.

We wandered toward the East Village; it's not a long walk when you're levitating. The East Village has a lot of the old ethnic neighborhood mixed in with the punk-hip-avant-garde scene. The Ukrainian Museum, the Blue and Gold Tavern, and then Surma. . . .

Going into Surma was like dropping out of New York for a while. In the dim, small store, Ukrainian music was playing. A rack displayed Ukrainian newspapers and books. Kim browsed through the embroidered blouses and tablecloths.

There was a shelf of wooden eggs decorated in

the same intricate geometric patterns that they paint on real eggshells at Easter time.

"*Pysanky*," I said.

"What?"

"*Pysanky*. The Easter eggs. That's what they're called."

"How do you know that?"

"I don't know, I heard it somewhere."

"Honestly, you know about so many different things."

We came out into the bright sunshine.

"Did you ever see Fabergé eggs?" Kim asked. "There are some at the Forbes Galleries. You know, right down the street from my house? Fabergé made a special one for the czar every Easter. They're gold with the most fabulous jewels and things inside. I'd love to be a czarina."

"Kimorova O'Harovich, empress of all the Russias."

"Easter's my favorite holiday."

"Why Easter?"

"Well, it's about rebirth and—What's yours?" she asked.

"I don't know. Halloween, I guess. When I was a kid, I'd go in the Village parade. My dad has a lot of artist friends; they hang out at Cecilia's all the time, and they'd fix up incredible costumes for me. Did I ever tell you my dad was an artist, before the restaurant? He met my mom at the Art Students League. Anyway, Cecilia's would be jumping, one big party, and I'd stuff myself with all the candy . . . I used to stick candy corn on my teeth, for monster teeth. Did you ever do that?"

I was telling her every single thing about myself. She seemed so interested; it was like she thought every detail was wonderful.

We headed west along Astor Place.

When you don't know someone, you think they're one particular way. Back in junior high, she never got silly like the other girls. What I'd thought was optimum cool turned out to be reserve. But she could be warm and gentle and I kept seeing different sides, a new turn of the kaleidoscope each time I was with her.

She squeezed my arm. "I love hanging out with you."

I was full of good feelings. I wanted to treat her to something, but my cash situation was pretty desperate. There was always Cecilia's. . . .

"How about brunch at my dad's place?" I said. "We do a nice brunch."

"Sure," she smiled.

I made a game of keeping her out of the stores along the way. I lost control on Greenwich Avenue—

she made me stop at Star Struck to look at the vintage clothing. Girls really love shopping!

I was proud to walk into Cecilia's with Kim on my arm. Even Bob the bartender, who was usually catatonic, stared at her. We took a front table where Ellen was on duty, and I introduced them. My *girlfriend*, Kim O'Hara, I said. Ellen was an NYU student with long, curly blond hair and a fantastic body; I used to have a crush on her and she thought I was just a kid. Part of me still wanted to impress her; I was pleased when she gave me the thumbs-up sign behind Kim's back.

Ellen smiled at me and waited, pencil poised over the order pad.

Kim studied the menu. "I can't decide. What are you having?"

"French toast Cecilia is the best," I told her, "with grated orange rind and Grand Marnier sauce, and *andouille*—that's creole sausage."

"That sounds wonderful," Kim said.

"It's my favorite too," Ellen said. And then she brought us a couple of mimosas. Cecilia's is very strict about serving underage kids, but Ellen was always inclined to help romance along, and a little champagne in orange juice was just the right touch of festivity.

"Thanks, Ellen," I said.

"My pleasure." She winked; subtlety isn't her strong point. "French toast, coming right up."

Kim and I clinked glasses. "To us," I said.

"To us," she repeated.

Kim was looking around, looking happy; she had a glow about her. I was proud of Cecilia's too. The tablecloths were starchy white and there was a bud vase with a red zinnia on each one. All that starchy white against the dark wood walls, not too crowded, art on the walls, the contented murmur of people eating delicious things—Dad was always saying it had ambience.

"Those paintings are my mother's. The watercolors."

Kim studied them with interest. "I like her work. It's good quality."

"Dad says she was very good, but she died too young to be recognized. I don't know enough about art to know for sure."

"They're excellent paintings, Andy. They're very subtle and fine."

I liked the way Kim seriously considered things and had real opinions. And I liked the way the corner of her mouth dimpled as she talked.

"I wish I'd known her, but I was only a baby. The restaurant's named for her; her name was Cecilia. I've seen lots of photos, but . . . You must remember your real mother. Birth mother, whatever you call it."

"No, I don't remember anything."

"Nothing? But weren't you about three when she—"

She interrupted. "I just told you, I don't remember anything."

I was surprised. I could remember back to when I was three, at least some things. Well, different people have different memory spans.

"We should have dinner here sometime," I said. "Give you a taste of my soul food."

"What's your soul food?"

"Chicken *paprikás*, *lekvar*. . . . Dad's the Hungarian half of Cecilia's. He was only a kid when he came over, but he can still speak Hungarian; all I know is a couple of choice words. I guess the last part of a culture that stays with you is the food. What's your soul food?"

"Mine?" She hesitated. "Ummm . . . corned beef and cabbage."

I laughed. "That's the O'Hara part."

"We don't really sit around eating corned beef and cabbage. Only when we have a St. Patrick's Day party. We eat regular food. Oh, and sometimes Mom makes things from Julia Child's cookbook."

"I meant Vietnamese specialties. Soul food is childhood memories."

"I can't think of anything."

"What about Vietnam, the country? What do you remember?"

"Not much. Nothing."

I swear I could see a screen dropping over her face.

Then she smiled brightly as Ellen approached. "Oh, that looks wonderful. I'm starving!"

She's not volunteering anything, I thought. We'd been chattering about a million different things, but about the most personal thing Kim had said all day was that she liked Easter.

Kim ate very strangely. She cut everything on her plate in half. She ate one half and pushed aside the other.

I admit I wolfed down my French toast. I looked at the untouched halves on Kim's plate.

"Don't you like it? If you want something else—"

"No, it's delicious! I always do that. I only eat half of everything and that way I won't gain weight."

I laughed. A lot of girls are peculiar about food. Moira at BT puts her hamburgers between paper towels and squeezes all the juices out. Sitting next to her at lunch is not a joy.

"You're nowhere near fat," I said.

"I know, but I won't take that chance."

"What if you *love* something—"

"I love this, I really do."

"If you love something, don't you ever gobble up the whole thing? I bet you do."

"No."

"Or three-quarters?"

"No, I eat exactly half."

"Even if it's something incredibly chocolaty?"

"Mmmm-hmmm."

I laughed. "Well, you can always fudge it by starting off with gargantuan portions."

"Gargantuan? I love your vocabulary."

"I love your eating habits."

She was laughing too. "Well, I don't get *gargantuan* portions."

"That's very disciplined of you."

"Your vocabulary is why I noticed you back in junior high," she said. "I really liked that."

"My *vocabulary*?" I wished she'd said more about my good looks or devil-may-care charm.

"You're going to do so well on the SATs. I bet you get eight hundred on the verbal part," she said.

"The SATs? How did that come up? They're two years away!"

"It's never too early to prepare. If I learn a page of the dictionary every week, then in two years I'll—"

"Memorizing the dictionary is the weirdest—"

"One page a week makes fifty-two a year," she said, "so in two years, I should know a hundred and four."

I laughed. "That should get you through the As."

Kim frowned. "That's not enough, is it? If I could do two pages a week—"

"That's crazy," I said. "Words are supposed to be about communication. You can't sit around memorizing dictionaries!"

"You don't understand," Kim said. "There are kids at Bronx Science who are geniuses. I'm not."

"So you're not a genius. Neither am I. So what?"

"I think you're brilliant!"

"No, wait, maybe I'm good with words, but I'm far from—"

"You *are* brilliant, but you don't try hard enough," Kim said. "I expected you to be much more ambitious."

"Look, I'm having a good time."

"That's an excuse for laziness," she said. But she reached for my hand and smiled. "I want to be a good influence on you."

Ellen interrupted us with the coffee. At Cecilia's,

it's made with a trace of chicory and Kim liked it. Then I ordered *crème brulée*, and Kim ate her *whole* portion. It was great to see her self-control finally crumble. I teased her about that for a while.

"I want to be a bad influence on you," I said.

The tip of her tongue flicked out to pick up the last of the cream. "Well, you're doing a good job of it."

"I promise I'll love you even if you get fat."

She glowed. "Will you? I love you, Andy."

I hadn't meant to tell her I *loved* her. I'd been kidding and it just slipped out. I liked being with her, I liked looking at her, and God, I wanted her. *Love* is such a heavy-duty word; it made me nervous. But I could see she was waiting for it, I guess it's what you're supposed to say to your girlfriend, and I was feeling all this warmth for her. . . .

"I love you too," I said.

Between laughing and talking, brunch stretched on and on.

"This was the nicest day," Kim said. "I love Cecilia's."

I played with her hand on the tabletop. "We should make it our Saturday morning tradition."

"That's so romantic, our own tradition." She smiled. "What are we going to pick for our song?"

"You don't *pick* a song. It has to be playing when

something special happens." I knew exactly the something special I was thinking of; I'd have a stereo in my round room and . . . I couldn't stop my mind from running in that direction, no matter how hard I tried.

"Well, I hope we get our song soon." Her hand curled around my finger.

Me too, I thought.

I was doing my homework at the table, trying to find exactly the right word, when Lorraine interrupted my train of thought.

"We're on a very tight . . . schedule," Lorraine said.

There was a strange rhythm to her speech because she was stretching on the barre set up in the living room. Though she takes a daily dance class, she works out most evenings too. She had her leg up along the barre and was bending her body over it. Then she straightened up, inhaled, and did it all over again.

"Jack is giving up his place at the . . . end of October, so we'll have . . . to be out by . . . then."

That's Cajun Jack, my dad's partner in Cecilia's. He was taking our apartment because it's so convenient, right over the restaurant.

"While the plumber's working upstairs . . . tomorrow, we could be knocking down walls."

"Sure. Sounds like fun," I said.

One final stretch and Lorraine sank to the floor. She sat cross-legged, wiping her face with a towel. "We have to get organized. As soon as the wallpaper comes off, we'll paint and then scrape the floors. We should do the bedrooms first, so at least we'll have someplace to sleep."

"Good idea," I said. "What's another word for puzzle?"

"Puzzle? What are you writing about?"

"A character sketch for short story. . . . Wait, I've got it! *Mystery*. No, *enigma*. *Enigma*. 'Under the smooth shell, there is an enigma. . . . there lurks an enigma. . . .' "

"What shell?" Lorraine said.

"We're supposed to relate someone we know to a fairy-tale character. Because fairy tales are full of universal symbols."

I chewed on my pencil. Maybe Kim wasn't exactly an enigma, but there was nothing wrong with adding a little pizzazz. Anyway, it's a good word. I guess I've always liked fooling around with words, getting the exact shades of meaning. *Miasma and paroxysm* used to be my favorites; they were hell to slip into conversation, though.

Under the perfectly beautiful, perfectly smooth shell, there lurks an enigma. Everything about her seems ideal. She's smart, pretty, has nice clothes, a nice family, a nice home, everything a teen-age girl could want. She has poise and self-control. She'd be the perfect Miss America. But her control is so rigid, and she holds on to it so hard; maybe she's terrified and more fragile than anyone suspects. If that thin eggshell shatters, will she ever be able to put the pieces together again?

I reread what I'd written. I couldn't tell if it was good or overblown; Mark would let me know. He always put red-ink chicken scratches all over my papers. "Cliché!" was one of his favorites. I was learning a lot from him.

Kim, *terrified*? That was out of left field; I'd gotten carried away, dramatizing. I had a funny feeling about it, though. Sometimes you don't know what you think until you write it down. Sometimes writing takes on a life of its own and sends you a message. If all the king's horses and all the king's men couldn't put Kim O'Hara together again . . . Why didn't I pick Sleeping Beauty or Cinderella? Or I could have written about Dad or Garrity or . . .

"Andy?"

"What?"

"Can you be at the house right after school tomorrow? To start work? We have to really *work*."

"Okay, Wicked Stepmother," I said. "No problem."

The plumber was a little rabbit of a man. His face was dead white, and big, pointed ears stuck out from under his Mets cap. He was putting the toilet into Lorraine and Dad's bathroom upstairs while we started on the dining room.

Dad had the sledgehammer. "Okay, here goes." He hauled off at one of the partition walls and, with a loud crash, pieces flew down. White dust billowed into the room.

"You know what I can't figure out?" Lorraine wiped dust from her mouth. "Why would anyone have done this? I mean, dividing a room into all these little compartments?"

"Let me have a turn!" I grabbed the sledgehammer.

Dad laughed. "Okay, go!"

I hauled off and hit what was left of the wall. Another shattering crash and the rest of it collapsed. "Hey, this is great!" How often does anyone get a chance to legitimately smash things? Working on the house was going to be a breeze.

"Whoa! Whoa!" The plumber had appeared at the top of the stairs and was yelling down at us. "What are you people doing?"

Lorraine stepped over the debris. "Taking down the walls."

"The walls! You're taking down the walls? I'm working upstairs and you're taking down walls? The second floor could collapse! And the third floor! And—"

"Don't worry, none of them are structural supports," Dad said. "Our engineer checked."

"But you don't know!" The pitch of his voice rose. "Remember the house on Twelfth Street last year? There was demolition next door and the whole house collapsed in a second. Oh, no, I'm not working where there's demolition."

"These are superficial partitions," Dad said. "The only structural support besides the outer walls is the one in the middle of the top floor."

"What? My room? In the middle of my room?" I said.

The plumber's nose twitched. "That dust. Is that asbestos dust?"

"Definitely not," Dad said wearily. "It's only plaster."

"Oh, no." The plumber shook his head. "Oh, no. My union won't let me work under dangerous conditions."

"Oh, please," Lorraine said. "There's nothing dangerous here."

"Dad? What about the wall in the middle of my room?"

"I'm leaving, lady," the plumber said.

"Please, you've got to finish," Lorraine pleaded. "All right, we'll stop. We'll stop right now."

He looked down at us suspiciously.

"We have to pick up, anyway," Dad said. "That's all we're going to do now. Clean up."

The plumber paused, drunk with power, while the three of us forced appealing smiles.

"Okay," he finally said. "Okay." He grumbled his way back upstairs. "Crazy people," he muttered.

Dad started gathering chunks of wall. "Let's get these out of the way. Give us room to work tomorrow." His hair was covered with a layer of white. "Give me a hand, Andy."

I dragged a piece toward the pile. "What about the wall in the middle of my room?"

"Oh. That one's structural. It holds up the roof."

"It what? It what? You mean it can't come down?"

"That's right."

"But what about my round room?"

"Andy, you'll have two demirounds instead," Lorraine said cheerfully. "One half for sleeping and maybe one for study."

"But how's my round bed going to fit?" I wailed.

"Maybe you could find a half-moon bed some-where." She gave me a big smile. "That would be very nice."

I looked at Lorraine. No, she'd never trade rooms with me. No point in trying. She was fixated on the fireplace. And no matter what I said, I'd always be outvoted two against one.

We bagged the small pieces, piled up the big ones, and carried the debris out to the trash. It took three trips. I tasted plaster dust in my mouth. We looked around the room. One wall down, one more to go.

"See, doesn't it look better already?" Lorraine said. "I wish we could finish!"

We listened to the clink of pipes from upstairs.

Dad was brushing dust from his jeans. "I'd better change and get back to the restaurant."

"Okay," Lorraine said. "I know what. I'll scrub out the kitchen and, Andy, you could start on the wall-paper upstairs."

"Sure. I'll start in my room and work my way down."

Lorraine took the scraper out of the tool box and handed it to me. I looked at its four-inch blade. I wasn't really going to need this thing, I thought. I was going to grab onto a piece of wallpaper near the ceiling—well, maybe I'd use the scraper to get started—and just peel it off. In big strips. Piece of cake.

That's not the way it was.

It didn't peel.

I scraped and scraped and scraped some more, and managed to dislodge only half of one monkey's tail. And under that, there was something faded pink and vaguely floral.

I found Lorraine in the kitchen. "It's not coming off."

"Get a sponge and wet it down first. That might help."

"Lorraine, there's something underneath. More wallpaper."

"Well, get all of it off." Sweat was making lines in the white dust on her forehead. She was scrubbing several centuries of grease from the walls. "And, Andy, be careful. Make sure you don't nick the plaster."

"Oh. Right. Okay."

I went back upstairs, past the *clink-clink-clink* of the plumber on the third floor. I hopefully soaked a patch with the sponge. And I scraped. And scraped. Blisters formed between my thumb and my index finger. The colors of mustard and lime and pink swam before my eyes. It seemed like hours went by before I had removed one lone monkey. I needed a break. I sat down on a windowsill and desperately stared at about a thousand more cavorting simians. I closed my eyes and they were still prancing under my eyelids. No way, I thought. No way.

I looked out of the window. The historical tour was gathered on the sidewalk. Terrific, a diversion. I ran downstairs.

"Lorraine! Remember, I told you we're on the landmarks tour? They're outside right now!"

"They are?" Lorraine looked exhausted.

"Right in front."

She dropped her scrub brush—with great relief, I thought. "We ought to go out and hear what they say."

"Yeah, let's!"

It wasn't that easy for us to blend in with the group—we were haggard and filthy—but except for an elderly woman who edged away from us, everyone's attention was on the leader.

". . . was originally built by Captain Junius Hagedorn. During New York City's yellow fever epidemic of 1804, the wealthy moved to the Village, to the 'country,' so to speak, in order to escape the crowded areas of disease, and Captain Hagedorn was among them. Exactly why he built on such a narrow strip is unknown; perhaps he considered it temporary housing. Carlyle Hagedorn took possession in 1890. Apparently pride of ownership took over: Notice the rosette carvings under the third floor windows."

Everyone gazed up.

"Of course, the Edna St. Vincent Millay house at seventy-five-and-a-half Bedford Street, at nine and a half feet wide, is the narrowest in New York. This Hagedorn house is most probably second."

"Where did the Russian influence come from?" an earnest woman asked. "The onion dome?"

The leader shrugged. "Carlyle Hagedorn had eclectic tastes. Notice the Gothic brickwork. The interior was reputed to be interesting. Unfortunately, after his death, the house passed on to a spinster daughter, was then sold out of the family, and eventually fell into disrepair. During the last decade, it became a notorious bordello known as Polly Lou's. . . ."

Lorraine and I looked at each other. Her eyes had widened. I choked to keep from laughing.

". . . and under those circumstances, it is unknown how much of the original interior remains."

Lorraine's face was pink.

"We will proceed to Commerce Street, to an out-standing example of . . ."

The group moved on.

"Polly Lou's!" I laughed.

Lorraine passed her hand over her eyes. "He did say we have Gothic brickwork," she said weakly.

BY the next morning, one of my blisters was broken and oozing. I showed it to Dad and Lorraine at breakfast.

Lorraine put down her forkful of scrambled eggs. "That's not too appetizing, Andy."

"Sorry."

"Put a bandage on it," Dad said. "We'll get you some work gloves."

"But—," I started.

"The plumber should be through by this afternoon, so we can take down the walls," Lorraine said, "and Andy, you'll continue with the wallpaper—"

"But—," I said.

"And Lazlo, you and I should start getting the linoleum up, so maybe by the weekend—"

"But—," I said.

"What is it, Andy?" Dad was stirring sugar into his coffee.

"About the wallpaper. . . . I have soccer practice some afternoons and—"

"Do you have practice this afternoon?"

I couldn't lie with Dad looking right in my eyes. "Well, not *this* afternoon, but—"

"Okay, good. I won't let this interfere with your homework or soccer, but you have enough free time."

"See, the thing is . . ." They were looking at me and waiting while I swallowed a piece of toast. "The thing is . . . that wallpaper won't come off."

"It comes off," Dad said. "I know it's hard, but—"

"Can't we get a professional wallpaper-scraping person?" I said.

Dad put his coffee cup down. "No. We can't."

"Or an automatic scraping machine?"

"I doubt there is such a thing."

"It's going to take me forever," I said.

"It'll take as long as it takes," Dad said. "In the meantime, Lorraine and I can get other things done."

"Once you get the hang of it," Lorraine put in, "it'll be easier, you'll see."

"Well, I don't want to do it!" I blurted out.

There was an ominous silence.

"You made a commitment, Andy." Dad was suddenly too calm, in his barely fuming mode. "I expect you to see it through."

I concentrated on my plate.

"Responsibility is what makes a man. We're giving you a lot of freedom; we've respected the fact that you're growing up. If you don't want to be treated like a kid around here, then show some responsibility."

I hate being lectured at.

"It's your house too, you know," Lorraine added.

"I'm getting attached to those monkeys," I said. "Why can't we leave them?"

"No," Dad said. "You took on an obligation. A man fulfills his obligations."

Hell, couldn't I still be a kid once in a while? Hadn't he ever heard of child labor laws? Dad was a great guy in a lot of ways, but there were times when I knew better than to argue with him. His set face and his unnaturally calm voice told me this was one of those times.

For once, I was eager to leave for school. School was the only escape hatch left from menial slavery.

There was a tenth-grade meeting called for that morning. That meant short story was canceled. Why didn't they ever have meetings during math?

We all filed into Room 22.

"What's this one about?" I asked The Redhead.

"Could be anything." She shrugged. "I hope Howie's not going to talk about Tenth-Grade Anxiety."

"What?"

"Last year we had to hear about Ninth-Grade Anxiety. It was terrible. It made all of us feel so—so *anxious*!"

There was no sign of Howie. Muffy seemed to be in charge. When we had settled into our seats, she started.

"We're going to discuss community service this morning," she said. "You know that's part of the BT philosophy and a BT requirement. Your service to the less fortunate of your city will be once a week, after school hours, one credit per semester, and I hope you'll pitch in enthusiastically. All of you at BT are lucky to be among the privileged, and we believe that gives you a responsibility."

I wasn't all that privileged compared to some of the others; Keisha's dad was a famous musician and Tom's dad was in the paper all the time with spectacular real estate deals and spectacular engagements, though Tom expressed himself by wearing rags. Anyway, it seemed like a decent idea and I listened, interested.

"This won't be busywork; you'll really be helping. There are two options; sign up for the one that seems most suited to your interests and abilities. First, renovation of an abandoned building to create apartments for the homeless. That's construction work, painting, spackling, whatever—"

I groaned out loud and everyone looked at me.

"Anything wrong, Andy?" Muffy looked concerned.

I shook my head.

"All right. Let's see, I was talking about construction. That's probably most appropriate for the physically stronger." She looked at me meaningfully. "Your other option is the soup kitchen at Saint Monica's. Making sandwiches, coffee, and soup, serving the homeless, cleaning up—basically doing whatever is necessary. One night a week of dinner service."

Oh, God, I thought. As if I hadn't had enough dinner service at Cecilia's!

"So write your name on one of the sign-up sheets and we'll work out the schedules. Please jot down any day that you're absolutely not available."

While everyone else was busy signing up, I went to talk to Muffy.

"I think this is great," I said. "I'm totally willing—but isn't there anything else I could do?"

"What's the matter, Andy?"

"There's an awful lot of construction and restaurant in my life already," I said.

"Oh?"

"I do want to pitch in." I meant that; I saw more homeless on the streets every day and *someone* had to help. "I just thought—maybe there's something else I can do. Anything else."

"Well, if you really have a problem with this . . . ," she said dubiously.

"I do," I said. "I'm in real danger of being burnt out by construction and restaurant."

". . . you could possibly join the eleventh graders. One of their options is tutoring children at the homeless shelter on Avenue A."

"That sounds fine."

"Helping them with their homework or reading. One evening a week, from seven to nine. They need more people badly."

"Terrific! I like that!"

"All right, good enough. I'll set it up."

Working with kids at a homeless shelter would be a worthwhile thing to do. I didn't like asking special favors, but I knew any more construction would turn me into a raving maniac.

So guess what I was doing after school? Scraping. With a bandage and work gloves. An inch at a time. I remembered reading somewhere that some colors induce nausea. I'm pretty sure they're mustard and lime green.

After a while, I sort of got into the swing of it. When I held the scraper at a certain angle. . . . I'll admit there were moments of mild triumph when a decent-size strip peeled away.

We had been reading *Zen and the Art of Motorcycle Maintenance* for American lit. It's good. I need to reread it; I didn't completely understand it the first time through, but it talks about doing a job the Zen way. Being in the moment, wholeheartedly, with pride in craftsmanship. It's all in the mental attitude.

I tried to adjust my attitude and scrape Zenfully.

The worst part was that it was deadly boring. Even plugged into my Walkman, the monotony got to me.

There had to be a way out of this.

I thought of good old Tom Sawyer whitewashing the fence. He made it seem so entertaining that he got all the neighborhood kids to do the job for him.

There had to be a way.

And then I got a brainstorm. I'd throw an all-day wallpaper-scraping party! A huge party, with my new friends from BT and my old friends from junior high. With big pots of food from Cecilia's. And music— Jo-Jo had a boom box and some great tapes. One scraper per person. I'd ask everyone to bring one along, and I'd buy some more just to be sure. Twenty, thirty people, figure four square feet per person, hopefully more if we had some ambitious workers.

Around noon, so there'd be daylight to scrape by; the lighting in the house at that point was some bare, dim bulbs. Saturday would be good. I made a lot of calls that night. I invited the BT kids at school the next morning. Everyone thought it would be a blast. Everyone was coming. I was nothing less than brilliant.

JANET Mayer, a BT eleventh-grader, and I were standing on the corner of Fourteenth Street and Seventh Avenue on Tuesday night, waiting for the car service.

"I don't get it," I said. "It isn't that far. We could get there by ourselves."

"I know," Janet said, "but the shelter can't have any of their volunteers getting mugged. Parts of Alphabet City are bad."

I shrugged. I liked to think I could take care of myself anywhere, but I guess the shelter people knew their own neighborhood.

"Is this your first time too?" I asked.

"Mmm-hmm. I'm kind of nervous."

A skinny man carrying a handful of gold chains stopped in front of us. "Fourteen karat. They're hot," he said. I shook my head no. He continued along the crowded sidewalk. "Fourteen karat," he called to the people going by. "Snatched 'em myself!"

Horns honked and traffic whizzed by us. A car pulled up to the curb. There was a twentyish guy in a suit and tie in the back. We got in next to him.

We introduced ourselves; his name was Frank.

"It's a good thing you're coming tonight," he said. "We're short. The other Tuesday volunteer has some kind of overtime project; she can't make it for a while."

"Were we supposed to get dressed up?" I asked.

"This?" He fingered his tie. "No. No, I was running late, didn't have time to change after work. You're better off in old clothes. The kids'll be all over you."

"All over us?" Janet said nervously.

"You'll see," he said.

The car let us off on Avenue A. The shelter was a squat building that took up most of the block. Its gray cement was covered by years of graffiti. On one side, there was a parking lot bordered by dented garbage cans. There were stores across the street, but I couldn't tell what kind; they were all shuttered with heavy metal gates. To the right, there was a windowless, burned-out building. A line of barbed wire along the sidewalk wouldn't have been a surprise.

Frank led us inside.

"This way." Janet and I followed him through the long hall, past a man and two women leaning against the wall. They stared at us.

The place smelled like a combination of disinfectant and something rotting.

"This is a family shelter," Frank said, "for people with children. It's a Tier One."

"A what?" I asked.

"That's the way the system is set up. Tier One is barracks-style. It's supposed to be temporary housing, for no more than one month. They're supposed to be moved up to Tier Two, which means a separate room per family, and then, hopefully, Tier Three, a subsidized apartment. The problem is, there's no space anywhere, so some of the families stay on and on here."

There was a noisy group clustered at the far end of the hall, mostly young kids, squirming and bouncing off the walls. As we inched past, a boy called, "Hey, teach! Let us in!"

"In a minute," Frank said. He opened the door and quickly closed it behind us. We entered a shabby room filled with tables and chairs and one decrepit couch with stuffing coming out. A small TV hung from the ceiling in one corner.

"The rec room," Frank said. "No adults are allowed in while we're using it with the kids. We get some resentment; you know, people want to watch TV and they get mad at being kept out, but—Mrs. Cannon, two new ones for you!"

A large, frazzled black woman came toward us.

"Great!" she said. "We're so shorthanded."

As we went through the introductions, there were loud bangs at the door.

"It's almost time," she explained. "A couple of rules: No kids under five; this is supposed to be tutoring. Sometimes the little ones try to sneak in and it's hard, but we've got to keep them out. And a parent has to check the child in and stay on the shelter premises while the child is with you. You'll get kids trying to come in who haven't been checked in and you can't allow that."

"We can't allow them in?" I said.

"There's a reason. We're not heartless." She looked worn-out. "We can't let this be used as a babysitting service while mothers are out on the street making crack deals. We try to encourage parental responsibility."

"Oh," Janet said.

"Addicts aren't in the majority here," Mrs. Cannon said quickly. "We have families who've been burned out of their apartments, teenage girls with babies and no place to go, the unemployed with no skills, women abandoned by the fathers of . . . People without safety nets. Many of them want more than anything for their kids to do well in school. You'll see. Some don't know or they're too beaten down by the system or . . ."

I was suddenly embarrassed by the way I was dressed. I hadn't thought. My jeans were faded and strategically ripped, that year's hot look. Faux poverty.

"Try to get the kids to do their homework," Mrs. Cannon went on. "If they won't, try to get them to read, or read to those who can't. We have a few books. . . . " She indicated a makeshift crate bookcase with her head.

I hoped I could handle this. I didn't know what to expect.

"I'm teaching a GED class next door, so if you have any problems . . . Anyway, Frank knows the ropes." She started for the door and then turned back to us. "Thanks for coming. I hope you'll stay with it and come every Tuesday. We need you."

Then the door was opened, kids came pouring in,

zillions of them, and I became too busy to sort out my impressions. There was the little boy who ran around the room being an airplane and wouldn't do anything else. There were the two junior high kids who sat on the couch and read comic books. There was Desirée, a cute second-grader with intricately ribboned pigtails, who zipped through her math with me.

"That's terrific," I told her. "You're very smart."

She gave me a shy, shiny-eyed smile.

"You must be awfully good in school."

"Uh-huh. I liked my old school. Back in the Bronx."

"How about your new school?"

She tucked her chin into her shoulder.

There was Luther, a natural charmer, who kept jumping on my shoulders whenever I tried to work with someone else. I told him to stop, but he kept right on. He kept bouncing on me all evening; I couldn't be strict with him.

There was the quiet, well-behaved fourth-grader, who willingly pulled out his reader. He stared with fierce concentration at the printed page, trying hard to break the code. He was Haitian; he didn't know a word of English.

A little girl was curled up in Janet's lap, sucking

her thumb, while Janet read a storybook to a small group. Frank had kids hanging from his arms. And everywhere, calls of "Teacher! Hey, teach!"

There was a pervasive odor of urine.

I worked with Nicole on her reading homework. She was at least nine. She'd say a few of the easy words and then quickly spell out the letters of others. "The boy doubleyou-ee-en-tee to the ess-tee-oh-are-ee and . . ."

"Wait, try to sound out the letters. *Sssst*—"

She rushed on. "I can read!" I think she honestly believed that. I didn't know what I was supposed to do.

"Come on, Nicole. *Sssst*—Store."

What about her real teachers, I thought. Were they passing her through school like that?

"Teach! Come here, teach!"

"Yo, turn on the TV!"

"I gotta finish the homework or my mama gonna smack me upside the head!"

"We're going to Tier Two! The case lady said!"

"Where the potato chips at? Last time there was potato chips."

A young boy sat at a table, drawing horses galloping on grass. He had only three broken crayons to work with, but you could see those horses moving.

"That's a terrific picture," I said.

"I know . . . Yeah, if I had a blue crayon, the sky wouldn't be yellow."

"It's coming out great, anyway. You're *good*!"

He nodded. "I know."

I watched as he added some crayon strokes for a flying tail. Maybe there were potential Picassos stuck in homeless shelters. Next week I'd bring in a brand-new box of crayons for him—if he was still here. I reminded myself that this was a transient population.

The two hours whizzed by, and the car service picked us up.

"They're great," Janet said. "Just like any other kids."

"Well, what did you expect?" I asked.

"I didn't know."

"Sure, they're just like any kids, except they don't have homes," Frank said. "It's roughest on the teenagers—no privacy at all, ever. No place to look in the mirror by yourself, or cry, if you feel like it. No place to be alone. Upstairs, it's rows of beds with men, women, and children all mixed up. Families don't necessarily get beds together. Depends on what's available."

"We don't make much of a difference, do we?" I said. "If I could work with one kid, the same one every time, maybe—"

"Don't get attached to any one kid," Frank said. "You can't do that."

"That Matthew, the skinny black one?" Janet said. "He's so smart! He's interested in science, and he knows all about dinosaurs and—"

"The best you can do is praise and encourage. That means a lot to them," Frank said. "But stick to the schoolwork. Don't try teaching anything else."

"What do you mean?" I said. "Why not?"

"My friend Tony was running a summer program, taking them to Central Park for soccer, things like that. So he was around a lot and there was this little boy, Karim, nine or ten years old. Anytime Karim had a problem, he'd settle it with his fists. 'Fighting's no good,' Tony kept telling him. 'If someone does something to you, you don't have to *punch*. That's wrong. Use words instead.' Karim looked up to him and Tony kept reminding him. So, over time, Karim tried talking instead of fighting."

"Sounds good to me," I said. "Sounds like your friend got through to him."

"Karim's father came looking for Tony and gave him one hell of a beating—broken nose, split lip. 'What kind of shit you telling my boy?' he was yelling. 'You making my boy a chicken?' "

"Wow," Janet said. "Was he crazy?"

"Who knows? Maybe the father wasn't off-the-wall. Kids have to be tough to survive around here. All I'm saying is, your values might not fit their reality."

Muffy was right, I thought. All of us at BT were overprivileged. Here we were, being whisked through these desolate streets by a car service. Those little kids had to walk the very same streets to school every day.

BY the time Saturday rolled around, I wasn't sure the party idea was that brilliant. I was nervous. What if the BT kids and my junior high group hated each other on sight? What if everyone just grimly removed wallpaper and had a rotten time? Or, what if they had such a great time that they never got around to scraping? That would be even worse.

Dad and Cajun Jack were okay with the food. There'd be a huge pot of goulash and noodles from Cecilia's. I bought paper plates, napkins, and plastic forks. So far, so good. Food was important. If the food was good, it couldn't be a *terrible* party. Could it?

No place to sit down except the floor, but that was okay.

Beer was a problem. Dad and Lorraine said definitely no. I knew some of the kids would be expecting beer. I'd been cultivating a cool image at BT; was I going to feel like a total jerk?

Dad got me a tub of ice that I filled with cans of soda. Twenty-odd people—God, that was a lot of sodas!~That was a lot of people! This was my first really big party; there'd never been enough room in the apartment.

"That's a lot of people," Lorraine said. "I'll be working downstairs, so it's up to you to see that no one gets too wild or damages anything." She looked worried. "You have to take responsibility."

What was this, Responsibility Month? That's all I'd been hearing.

A bunch of my junior high friends showed up first. Jo-Jo, Garrity, Lizabeth, Teddy, Marisa, Kate, Greg . . . Good, they were all wearing old clothes, sweats or old jeans, like I'd told them.

"Hey, Andy!"

"How's it going, buddy?"

"You're going to live here? It's neat!"

"God, that smells good! When do we eat?"

"I figured we'd eat," I said, "and *work*, and then eat some more, and *work*, and—"

A soft "Hi," and Kim was in the doorway in her idea of work clothes: a perfectly pressed denim jumpsuit with embroidered pink flowers. She was carrying a ruffled pink apron. The jumpsuit hugged her perfect curves. I was proud of how pretty she was.

"You all know my *girlfriend*, Kim O'Hara."

"Sure. Hi, Kim."

The girls didn't greet her with hugs and squeals, the way they do when they haven't seen each other for a while. There were polite hellos. So Kim hadn't been best friends with the girls in junior high. So what?

"You guys are going out?" Marisa asked.

Kim and I smiled at each other.

"No kidding! Since when?" from Kate.

"Uh . . . September," I said.

"September eighth," Kim said.

Then a BT bunch came in, led by The Redhead.

"This is fabulous!" she said. "This is the most interesting house! It is absolutely *great*!"

I glanced at Kim. She lowered her eyes.

The junior high group stood together. The BT group stood together. I started introductions, but The Redhead cut right through it. She made a beeline for Garrity.

"He's cute! Who *is* this? He's adorable!"

Garrity grinned through his blush. He was bowled over by her. Then everyone was laughing and the groups started mingling. Thank God for assertiveness, I thought. The Redhead had broken the ice.

We dug into the goulash, and Jo-Jo's boom box was blasting, and everybody was sitting around on the floor talking. More BT kids came in and a little later, more from junior high.

It was noisy, lots of conversation and Hammer. I saw Lizabeth from junior high flirting with Tom from BT. It was going to be okay.

When everyone looked happy and reasonably well-fed, I said, "So let's get to work."

"This is really different. I've never been to a *wall-paper* party before." That was Moira, BT's official club kid. She was always telling us about her weekends in endless detail. "Last night I went to this bash at the Gilded Cave and you should have *seen* who was there. I was wearing my—"

"Anybody need a scraper?" Great, a lot of kids had brought their own.

"I was wearing my gold lamé top, and it was so funny, because this guy with pink hair, no, it was fuschia, standing straight up on his head, it was so funny, anyway he said—"

"Moira, is this going to be a *long* story?" the BT bunch said in unison.

I was passing out work gloves. "Let's all do the

monkeys first, and then we can get to the bananas and grapes downstairs."

They enthusiastically attacked the simians, Moira chattering all the way.

"This doesn't come off that well," Jo-Jo said.

"It's all in the wrist action," Tom said.

"Andy, there are pink flowers underneath. Do we take off the pink flowers too?"

"Everything," I said happily. "Everything comes off. Just don't nick the plaster."

"It's all in the *body* action," Greg said. He was putting in hip thrusts in time to the rap.

"Yeah, that works!" Everyone started twisting and scraping and inventing new moves.

"It's the Wallpaper Walk!"

"It's the Funky Monkey!"

I worked next to Kim. She was frowning with concentration, scraping methodically.

This wasn't bad at all, I thought. This job had actually become doable.

A sound like a fingernail across a blackboard made me shudder.

"Stop!" Moira squealed. "I can't stand that!"

"I can't help it," Tom said. "It's the scraper."

"Ooooh, stop!"

"Hey Jo-Jo, turn up the box and drown him out!"

The music was blasting. I prayed Lorraine wouldn't come racing up. Nothing kills a party faster then a parent complaining about noise.

"Andy! Look!" Marisa yelled.

She was working at the wall in the center and we all rushed over. She had uncovered some kind of carving. We pulled the wallpaper off carefully. There was intricate wood molding all around the arch, a bas-relief of wheat and flowers.

"That's beautiful. That's really something!"

Must be old Hagedorn's touch, I thought. "Hey, careful with that." I'd clean it up and oil it later. This house was going to be fantastic. It was *mine*!

A little later, The Redhead exclaimed, "Come here, everybody! Look at this!"

We crowded around.

"Look what those two monkeys are doing! The ones under the leaf!"

The boys started racing around the room, looking for more monkeys in action. "How about these two!" The girls mostly giggled. There were a couple of blushes.

"Oh," I said coolly. "I noticed them before."

"Who in the world lived here?" Lizabeth asked.

"Polly Lou and the girls."

"What?"

"It was a bordello. Polly Lou's."

Everyone was laughing. "No kidding?"

"You ought to keep the wallpaper up," someone said. "It's a conversation piece."

"I think we should get it off just as quickly as possible," Kim said. She hadn't cracked a smile and everyone looked at her. "Let's get to work." Her voice rang out in the moment of quiet as the tape ended.

I followed her back to our section. "Loosen up, will you?" I muttered.

"There's nothing at all funny," she muttered back. "And I don't like that redhead."

"Come on, she's great! She has more personality—"

Kim gave me a searching look. "Do you really think so?"

I shrugged.

The Redhead was bouncing around the room, talking to everyone, scraping a little here and there. Garrity was desperately trailing after her.

"Hey, Redhead!" I called. "What's your real name?"

"You know. P. J. Farroday."

"Yeah, but what does the P. J. stand for?"

"Oh, nothing much."

"Come on, what is it?"

Other people got into it. "You have to tell! What is it? Come on, tell!"

"Okay, if you've got to know." She was laughing. "Are you ready for this? Prudence Jane."

Prudence! The misnomer of all time. I laughed. It would fit Kim, I suddenly thought. And then I felt disloyal. Kim was terrific. Kim was my girlfriend.

"Do you *like* her?" Kim said under her breath.

"Sure." I saw Kim's strained look. She was jealous! No one had ever been jealous of me before, and it was nice. I put my arms around her. "Only as a friend."

I kissed the tip of Kim's nose and she leaned against me.

"We'd better get back to work," she said after a while. "We have to set a good example."

"Right." I was smiling. Strips of wallpaper were piling up on the floor. Big patches of wall had been cleared.

Everyone worked along for a while. Then Moira and Teddy started dancing to a Prince tape. "Do the Funky Monkey!" Garrity yelled, "like the wallpaper guys!" Everybody was getting into dirty dancing.

I grabbed Kim's hand. "Come on."

"No."

Tom and Greg threw bits of wallpaper at the girls.

It floated like confetti. The tape ran down. There was plenty of goulash left, and people started helping themselves again.

"Andy, what makes this so good? My mother's doesn't taste anything like it."

"Authentic Hungarian paprika, and lots of it."

"Wish we had some beer."

I hesitated. "My dad said no." Everyone seemed to accept that. It was okay.

The Redhead, Jo-Jo, Keisha, and Teddy were sitting cross-legged on the floor. I sat down with them and soon everyone else drifted over. Except for Kim. I heard her *scrape-scrape-scrape*.

"I love parties in empty rooms," Lizabeth said.

"Right. Because they're so . . . empty." Jo-Jo said.

"I was at a bash last week," Moira started. "It was so crowded, you wouldn't believe, *everybody* was there, and I was wearing my black lace bustier, the one from Betsey Johnson; anyway, it was so funny, this guy said—"

"Moira, is this going to be a *long* story?" we all said in unison.

"What I meant about empty rooms . . . " Lizabeth continued. "It's like we're all sitting around a campfire."

"Except for Kim," Marisa said.

She was still at it.

"Hey, Kim!" I called. "Take a break."

"I'm finishing my patch," she said.

Scrape-scrape-scrape.

Everyone was watching her, industrious in her ruffled pink apron.

"She's just like that pink Energizer rabbit." The Redhead guffawed. "She keeps on going and going and going . . ."

They laughed and I was embarrassed. I got up and went over to Kim.

"Can't you give it a rest?" I led her toward the group. "Come on and join the party."

I must have sounded irritated, because Kim looked hurt and puzzled.

"I was doing it for *you*," she said softly.

We sat and talked for a while and then we worked some more, but daylight was fading. Jo-Jo and I went downstairs to the refrigerator and brought up the lemon tarts for dessert.

"From Cecilia's," I told them.

I turned on the bare bulb hanging from the ceiling, but it was too harsh. Everyone yelled at me to turn it off. They seemed happily tired and relaxed in the twilight. Lizabeth from junior high was in a heavy-duty clinch with Tom from BT. We hadn't gotten to the bananas and grapes, but the monkeys were just about gone and it had been fun too. The party was a smash.

Kim stayed behind after the last straggler had taken off.

"I'll help you clean up."

"That's okay. You don't have to."

"I want to. I won't leave you with this big mess."

We got big plastic garbage bags and swept up wallpaper and paper plates. She helped me carry down the pot of congealing goulash.

Kim was the only one who'd thought to stay and clean up. She was sweet and considerate, and she *really* liked me. Even loved me, maybe. So what if she didn't mingle that well with my friends? It was okay to be a little reserved. Or maybe she'd just taken the work more seriously for *my* sake. And she was certainly beautiful. Easily the most beautiful in the room. So what was wrong with me?

We filled more garbage bags with wallpaper and soda cans.

"Penny for your thoughts," Kim said.

"Oh. No thoughts," I said. "Just tired."

What was the matter with me? There was a guy who came into Cecilia's for dinner almost every night and never with the same woman twice. Blondes, brunettes, redheads—he romanced them all between the chicken *paprikás* and the pecan pie. Ellen called him "the Snake." He'd try to hit on Ellen too, and she'd keep saying things like, "Digested any rodents lately?" He's all screwed up, she told me; he's trying to prove something. I didn't want to be like him. But there were so many girls in the world . . .

"Your room will be wonderful," Kim said. "Especially with that molding. You were right. I had no imagination."

She sounded apologetic; it made me feel bad. "Well, it was a mess when you first saw it."

I'd had this big crush on Kim. A huge crush, all through ninth grade, before I even knew her. And now she was my girlfriend! So why was I watching The Redhead all afternoon? Hair the color of marmalade and a firecracker personality . . . And Lizabeth—she looked a lot better than she used to. Tan, blond, and *very* amorous with Tom . . . And Marisa, with the huge hazel eyes and the longest legs I ever saw . . . Moira was a ditz, but she had satiny skin over hourglass curves . . . I couldn't help wondering about them.

No, I wasn't anything like the Snake. He was a grown man specializing in one-night stands. I was a healthy, fifteen-year-old . . . *virgin*, God help me! It was sheer frustration that was making me berserk.

I liked the kids at the shelter, especially Roy. That was the fourth-grader I'd dubbed "the Artist."

We weren't supposed to favor anyone or bring something for just one kid. One Tuesday, Janet brought in a big bag of Fritos for everyone to share. They pounced on it, ripping the paper.

I couldn't afford a whole truckload of crayons; three jumbo boxes of Crayolas was the best I could do. The next week, I took them out of the paper bag at the table where Roy was sitting. Other kids grabbed for them, but I'd given Roy a head start on picking colors. He knew it too.

"Thanks, man," he said under his breath. He sneaked several into his jeans pocket.

Nobody could ever get him to touch his homework. All he wanted to do was draw.

"How about getting some work done?" I said.

"Naw, I don't feel like it."

"If you don't know math, how're you going to know what to charge for your paintings?"

He cocked his head. "I don't have no paintings."

"I'm talking about when you're a grown-up artist. And you'd better read and write well if you're going to deal with art galleries and stuff."

"You're connin' me," he said with a grin. He was putting fine, feathery leaves on a tree branch with the edge of a crayon.

Then a new kid pulled at my arm. "Come on, I want to show you . . ."

Later that evening, Roy came over to me. Nonchalantly, as if he'd just thought of it himself, he said, "Maybe I'm gonna crack this math. You want to help me?" I was elated.

I was telling Kim about it. We were at Dominic's on MacDougal, having pizza after the movies on Saturday night. I tried to ignore the way she was carefully cutting up her half-slice with a knife and fork.

". . . so maybe I'm doing some good," I was saying, "and if I keep on working with him—"

"I don't understand what you're so excited about," she said. "He still lives in a shelter. You're not changing his life."

"You should see him. He's talented and bright

and"—I took a bite, dripping cheese down my chin—
"hey, I have a great idea! Come with me next Tuesday
and see for yourself."

"No, I couldn't."

"Sure you could. They need volunteers and—"

"No."

"—and it's something we can do together. If we're
gonna have anything in common."

"What's that supposed to mean?" She looked hurt.
"Don't you think we have anything in common?"

"Well, sure, but—" I felt like I was walking on
eggs.

"We could do a million other things together."

"Right."

"I just don't like the homeless."

"You don't *like* them? How many homeless people
do you actually know?"

"You know what I mean. They're spoiling the
park, they're all over the streets, they rip up garbage
bags and leave a mess, they're ruining the whole city."

"Okay, true," I conceded, "there's a problem. So
the right thing to do is help."

"It's their own fault if they're on drugs or won't
work. They ought to be helping themselves."

What was I doing with Miss Ultra-Reactionary,
U.S.A.? "Wait a minute, there are all kinds of people
out there. It's not just—"

"Anyway," Kim said, "I don't want to. I don't have time."

"Well, make time, damn it!"

"What are you getting mad about?"

"I'm talking about *kids*, Kim. Come with me next Tuesday. Just once." I wanted to see her being warm and wonderful at the shelter. Janet had been nervous at first too. Maybe if we did this together, with both of us involved . . .

Kim looked upset. "Why is it so important to you?"

"Because it is!" I didn't know how to say it without saying too much. I like Kim. But ever since the party, I'd been thinking. We didn't share all that much.

"Are you mad about something?"

"No."

"Did I *do* something?"

"It's all the things you won't do."

"If you're talking about sex—"

"Not just that. You're like—so careful about everything. Can't you even get your hands greasy when you eat a pizza? You're so damn perfect!"

She looked down and pushed her plate away. I kept on eating, though I didn't feel like it anymore.

"I don't know what you want," she said. "I'm the way I am."

She was tearing at her napkin.

"I'm sorry," I said. "I didn't mean that. Eat any way you like."

She shrugged.

"The shelter would look good on your college applications," I said. It bothered me to know that was the best way to reach her.

She chewed on her lip.

"What I want—when I'm this enthusiastic, I think my girlfriend should at least be interested. Interested enough to come *one* time. That's not an earthshaking commitment, is it? *One* time. Otherwise, what's the point? What have we really got going here?" It came out harsher than I intended.

She looked stricken. I could see I'd hurt her, and I felt terrible. Why was I browbeating her about the shelter anyway? Whether she came or not wasn't a big deal. I didn't even know why I'd made an issue out of it.

There was a silence, and I didn't know what to say.

"All right," she said in a small voice. "I'll go with you."

She was forcing herself. And I realized how much she wanted to please me, and how badly she didn't want us to break up. I felt worse than terrible.

"Listen," I mumbled, "forget it. You don't have to."

She swallowed. "I said I'll go." Her napkin was in shreds.

On Tuesday evening, Kim and I followed Frank and Janet into the shelter. I had my arm around her; her shoulders were stiff.

In the hallway, we passed a group of teenage girls, girls no older than Kim, holding their babies. The babies were neat and beribboned and wearing little hats.

"It's like they're playing Barbie dolls . . . " I let my voice trail off. The tension on Kim's face stopped me.

"I was kind of worried the first time too," I said. "But you'll see . . .

"They'll call you teacher," I said. "That still strikes me funny. Me, a *teacher*!"

I was carrying a children's book, about the Impressionists, in a Barnes & Noble bag. I'd looked all over for some kind of art book for kids, and this was the only one I'd found.

"It says sixth-grade level, but that's not too far from fourth grade, is it? Anyway, Roy's smart. It can't be *only* for him, but—"

She wasn't listening to me. She looked frozen.

In the rec room, I introduced Kim to Mrs. Cannon. Mrs. Cannon was rushing off to her class, but she smiled and said, "Great! Thanks for coming!"

Kim's eyes darted around the room. Okay, I knew it smelled bad. I sure hoped she wouldn't notice any roaches. Okay, it wasn't exactly her kind of place, but—then the door opened and there was the on-slaught of kids.

A little girl grabbed Kim's hand. "You're pretty! Read my book with me!" Kim hesitantly allowed herself to be pulled toward a table. The kids would win her over, I thought, and she'd wind up having fun.

"Hey, teach!"

I looked around for Roy. No sign of him. Maybe he was late.

"Hey, teach, what's that?"

I tightened my grip on the paper bag. "Nothing." I put it in the coat closet with my jacket. I wanted Roy to have first dibs.

A lot of new faces, dozens of familiar ones. I got involved in the mysteries of long division with Carrie, while Luther bounced against my back. I saw Kim surrounded across the room. One of the girls was playing with her hair.

A little boy, crying, had squeezed himself into the corner. Janet was kneeling down next to him.

Frank broke up a wrestling match.

"Two into eight . . . " I said.

"Four!" Carrie yelled.

"Good. Now bring it down . . ."

"I'm good in math, right?"

"You're great! Bring down the zero and . . ."

No sign of Roy.

Luther and Jimmy chased each other around the room and Miranda showed me her spelling. The boy in the corner hadn't budged; Janet was trying to comfort him, but his face was pressed against the wall. Frank was reading to a group clustered around him.

"Teacher! Help me!"

"Yo, teach! Over here!"

Suddenly Kim was next to me. She had her jacket on. "I'm leaving." Her voice sounded choked.

"Wait, I—finish up, Carrie, and then show me." I followed Kim through the room. "What's the matter?"

"I have to go! I have to!"

"What? We can't—"

Her eyes were wide and panicked, stark in a pale face.

"Kim? What is it? Are you sick?"

She shook her head.

"The car doesn't come for another hour and— what happened?"

She made a move for the door.

I grabbed her arm to stop her. "Wait, I can't leave yet—they're shorthanded and—"

She pulled away from me. She bolted through the door and down the hall. I ran after her and gripped her shoulders.

"You can't walk these streets by yourself!"

She was breathing too fast. She bit her lip and took a deep breath before she could speak. "Yes, I can. I'll be all right."

"Kim, wait, I'll tell—"

"No. You stay."

People loitering in the hall looked at us curiously.

"I'm sorry. I'm sorry, I can't—" Tears welled in her eyes. "I'll find a cab."

I was shocked and torn in all kinds of directions at once. I didn't know what to do. As soon as I let her go, she ran down the hall to the main door. I watched, paralyzed, as she frantically rattled the knob. And then she ran out.

I started back to the rec room. The kids, I couldn't just walk out. She'd get a cab. It wasn't even eight o'clock. Cabs didn't cruise this neighborhood. I should never have let her go. Something was wrong. I shouldn't have let her go alone!

I turned and rushed through the main door. I didn't see her. I looked in both directions. I didn't know which way she went. I walked up the street. It was cold; my jacket was still hanging in the closet. Maybe she had found a cab. There had to be cabs.

I came back to the rec room. Carrie ran to show me the work she had done. I checked her answers. I went through Alex's reader with him.

What was wrong with Kim anyway, I thought. Spoiled brat behavior. So she didn't like it, but couldn't she have waited for me? I had a responsibility here. What was all the hysteria?

I tried whipping myself into anger, but all I could see was Kim's eyes, wide and panicked. All I could feel was guilt and worry.

High-pitched voices swirled around me. A set of twins chattered about rock stars. Little Alex jumped around, bragging in a singsong, "I'm the toughest and I'm the meanest, so don't mess with *me*!" Miranda curled herself next to me. "Was that your girlfriend?" she asked. "She was pretty. Are you going to marry her?"

I'd call her as soon as I got out of here. No, I'd go directly to her apartment. The look on her face and the way she ran out—it was a red emergency flag. We had to talk.

Time was up. The kids straggled out and Mrs. Cannon came in to lock up.

"Mrs. Cannon? Where's Roy tonight?"

"Roy?"

"The little boy who draws all the time."

"Oh yes. They've left."

"Left? Why? Where did they go?"

"Offhand, I'm not sure."

I hoped that meant moving up to Tier Two . . . That would be good news for Roy, but I couldn't help feeling bad. I put on my jacket and took the book out of the paper bag. I added it to the handful of torn books in the crate. Maybe someone else could get something out of it. And I tried to make myself believe Roy was in an apartment, with his own room and a desk and lots of crayons.

I went directly to Kim's house as soon as the car service dropped me off. I fidgeted while the doorman announced me; he was operating in slow motion. Finally I was in the elevator. I kept punching the twelfth-floor button, definitely in the category of stupid-people tics; I knew it wouldn't make the elevator go any faster, but I had to do something.

Mr. O'Hara answered the doorbell.

"Hi. Is Kim here?" I felt as I'd been running.

"Come in, Andy. She came home a while ago."

Okay. It was okay; she got home all right. I followed Mr. O'Hara into the living room.

"Sorry, I know it's late," I said. "I just want to talk to her for a minute."

"No problem."

Mrs. O'Hara and Tracey were watching TV.

"Did you and Kim have a big fight?" Tracey talked through a mouthful of brownie.

"Now, that really isn't your business, is it?" Mrs. O'Hara shook her head and smiled at me.

"I was just *asking*!" Tracey stared at me curiously. "She was acting *weird*."

"No," I said. "At least, I don't think so."

"She's taking the world's longest shower." Tracey licked chocolate crumbs off her lip. "As soon as she came from your house, she got right in the shower and she hasn't come out. Even though *Rear Window*'s on."

"From my house?" I said.

"Trace, why don't you go knock on the door and tell her Andy's here," Mr. O'Hara said.

"Wait, later." Tracey's attention was on the TV. "I want to see this part."

Mrs. O'Hara got up. "All right, I'll tell her."

"Andy, how about some coffee or cider or—" Mr. O'Hara asked.

"Coffee, if it's made anyway."

"I'm talking instant decaf," Mr. O'Hara said. "Is that okay?"

"Great," I said. "Thanks."

I was left alone on the couch with Tracey. "What did you say before, about my house?"

"Nothing. Andy, did you ever see this? It's *scary*. There's one part where they find the dog and—"

"Did Kim say we were at my house tonight?"

"Yeah. . . . Ooooh, he's sneaking up behind her! I can't watch!"

Kim never lied to her folks, not as far as I knew. She didn't need to; she never even stretched a rule, not with me anyway. So why did she lie about tonight?

Mrs. O'Hara came back into the living room. "She's coming right out." Then Mr. O'Hara was there with the coffee, and the three of them settled back to watch the movie.

I sneaked glances at their faces. Tracey was a good kid, kind of normally twelve-year-old obnoxious, nothing complicated. Mrs. O'Hara had an open, warm way about her, and Mr. O'Hara was a nice, low-key guy. Easy people to be around; next to them, the Szabos were hyperkinetic.

The movie was giving all the here-comes-the-killer signals—shadowed scene, nervous music. And I thought, what's really scary is when everything appears to be so normal, but . . . I studied Mr. O'Hara; he caught my glance and smiled at me. Tracey was stuffing her face with another brownie and Mrs. O'Hara said, "How about leaving some for Kim and

Andy?" Mr. O'Hara said something about Grace Kelly and how this was her best picture . . .

"Andy?" Kim was in the doorway, wrapped in a big white terry-cloth robe. A white towel was turban-style around her hair. Her face was calm now. A beautiful, controlled mask.

"Hi." I went toward her.

"I guess we can talk in my room." She wouldn't quite look at me.

"Are you guys going to *kiss* and *make up?*" Tracey made loud smacking noises.

"Behave yourself, Tracey," I heard Mr. O'Hara saying. And then Mrs. O'Hara's "you're embarrassing your sister," as I followed Kim down the hall.

I closed the door of her room.

"I'm sorry," Kim said. She looked every which way but at me.

The terry-cloth robe was oversize; Kim looked lost in its folds.

"I'm sorry too. I shouldn't have let you go alone," I said. "Did you find a cab?"

"It was all right. I went up to Tenth Street and took the crosstown."

"I was worried. I never should have—"

"You had to stay. It was all right. No one bothered me."

"Well, what happened? What was it all about?"

"I'm sorry, Andy. I tried, I really tried. I had to get out of there."

"Did someone say something? Did something happen?"

She shook her head.

"Well, how about explaining? I mean . . ."

She took the towel from her head. Her hair was wet and tousled. "Why do you need explanations? You just about forced me to go and I didn't like it. That's all."

"You just didn't *like* it?"

"That's right." Her face was shiny clean against the white.

"What were you doing in the shower all that time, scrubbing the shelter away?"

She hesitated and then nodded.

"All right, it's not that clean, but, jeez, I didn't think you'd turn out to be a princess! They're just kids."

"You *made* me go. I told you I didn't want to! It was awful. They're not just kids, they're *needy* in every way. They were pawing me, for attention, and— They're in trouble, and if you don't know that, you don't know anything. I couldn't—" She bit her lip and glanced at the door; she deliberately lowered her voice. "I couldn't stand being there."

She was too intense about it. Something was going on here that I didn't understand. "Kim, what—"

"Can we forget about it? Isn't there anything else we can talk about?" She faced the mirror over her dresser and ran a comb through her hair.

"Yeah, as a matter of fact, there is. Why did you lie to your folks?"

She whirled around. "*Lie?* What lie?"

"Tracey told me you said we were at my house."

"Oh, that. I didn't want to talk about the shelter. They would have asked, and I didn't want to get in a big conversation about it."

"Why not? I don't get it," I said.

She turned away. She played with the things on top of the dresser, moving perfume bottles around, opening and closing a jewelry box. "There's nothing to get. You're quizzing me too much. About every little thing."

I heard the eleven o'clock news starting and then Mr. O'Hara's voice. "Andy? It's a school night."

"I know, I'm going," I called.

I looked at the big stuffed panda on Kim's bed. I looked at the row of seashells on the windowsill, all neatly labeled. Kim mechanically combed her hair, her back toward me. Our eyes met in the mirror.

What was the matter with her anyway? She just didn't *like* the shelter? She owed me an explanation, damn it! I didn't need to put up with her tantrums. I thought of walking away; she was too complicated for me. But—her face in the mirror . . .

I went to her. "Are we going to kiss and make up, like Tracey said?"

"I wasn't mad at you," she said.

I turned her around. "Let's kiss and make up anyway."

Our lips touched. She put her arms around my neck and I could feel her body relaxing through the big, loose robe. She seemed so fragile and I felt tenderness for her wash over me.

"I want to be close to you," I murmured into her damp hair. "Tell me what's really—"

She pulled away. "There's nothing to tell."

She walked me into the living room. Tracey was sprawled on the comfortable, not-too-new couch. Mrs. O'Hara was picking up cups and plates from the coffee table. Mr. O'Hara asked if anybody had seen his glasses; he'd misplaced them again.

"They're on top of your head!" Tracey yelled.

Mr. O'Hara's hand went up and, of course, they weren't there.

"Got you!" Tracey yelled, and everyone laughed.

Kim too; maybe I was only imagining that her eyes were troubled. Mr. O'Hara put his arm loosely around Kim's shoulders and I said good night to everyone. The warm oranges and reds of the Persian rug glowed in the lamplight.

What's wrong with this picture?

LORRAINE was ecstatic. After months of running to auditions all over town, she finally got a part in a new off-Broadway show. It was a musical comedy based on *King Lear*, called *Oh, Daddy*!

"I'm Goneril," she burbled. "Not just a chorus dancer—I'm a major character."

Too quickly, she swung from pure joy to frenzied slave-driving. "The house has to be done before rehearsals get into full gear. So get to work!"

The party took care of the monkeys. I still had to face the bananas and grapes. I adjusted my attitude to a Zen frame of mind and started scraping an obvious seam.

"Lorraine!" I yelled. "A miracle!"

She came running upstairs. She'd been chipping

away at the living room linoleum and she looked battle-fatigued.

"What? What?"

"Look!" I showed her with a sweeping move. The whole damn thing was peeling off! She grabbed another corner, and in a couple of minutes we were grinning at each other over the huge curled-up sheets at our feet.

"Wonderful! Now you can help me with the linoleum!" she said.

For some insane reason, the linoleum had actually been nailed to the floor. There were nails to be pried up every six inches. Then, days of *chip-chip-chip*.

"I have a great idea," I said. "Let's give a linoleum party."

"Your friends can't be that dumb," she said, "and I can't stand any more rap."

The walls were bare, we finally got the floors cleared, and then it was time to paint.

"You don't really want your room black," Dad said.

"Why black, Andy? It'll be dark and depressing," Lorraine said.

"Of course, it's your room and your choice . . ." Dad started.

". . . but not *black*," Lorraine continued.

I clung to my vision of an all-black seduction special for a while, but I didn't truly want to live like a mole. What made it tough to change my mind was their constant "not *black*" refrain. It was hell to compromise my independence. I saved face by using it as a bargaining wedge.

"Maybe I'll *consider* not black," I said, "if I can definitely get black satin sheets."

"Black satin sheets?" Lorraine looked at me curiously.

Dad laughed. "All right, I suppose so."

So it was white paint. Days of white paint everywhere. Dad painted. Lorraine painted. I painted. Miles of white paint. I was snow-blinded by an avalanche of white.

We rented a floor-scraping machine. That thing was *heavy*. I helped Dad, and a couple of near-hernias later we got it up the spiral stairs. Floors were scraped. An edger finished—guess what—the edges. Dust flew. We sneezed. Then one coat of polyurethane. The smell woke up my sinuses. Another coat. Took forever to dry.

"Is a third coat *necessary*?"

"If we're doing it, let's do it right," Lorraine said, grimly.

Then one day we looked around, and suddenly the house was gleaming. Shining herringbone wood floors, fresh white walls, and sunlight streaming through the back windows. We polished the marble fireplaces and the hand-carved moldings. We washed years of dirt from the small stained-glass window by the front door, and a rainbow of colors reflected into the living room.

"It's beautiful." Lorraine sounded awed. She reached for Dad's hand.

"Our *home*," Dad said.

I threw my fists in the air. "We did it!"

There were still odds and ends to finish—replacing some cracked panes, caulking windows, pointing the brick—but we moved in.

The only home I'd ever known was the apartment over Cecilia's. I liked my new room, but on the first night I had a vaguely uneasy, at-loose-ends kind of feeling. The little noises the house made were different from the distinctive creaks in the apartment. I had to stop and think about where light switches were.

It was real trauma for our cat, Katie. She'd patrolled Cecilia's and the apartment—her territory—with a confident tail up. Here she slouched down and started at the least sound. She suspiciously sniffed the air. When she wasn't hiding under the bed, she moved in hesitant, restless circles, looking as grieved as a cat can look.

The next day, I hung my Springsteen, skateboarding, and Harley-Davidson posters on the wall; found the right spot for my tape deck and reconnected the speakers; and shoved my desk and typewriter in front of a window. I settled in. It took Katie longer. She zeroed in on a familiar pillow from home, a life raft in a sea of strangeness. Finally, she got around to rubbing against things to leave her scent and make them hers.

Even homeless people stuck to their familiar spots around the Village. One stringy old guy always slept on the steps of the Jefferson Market library, and he'd hang out just a couple of steps away, near Balducci's. An obese black woman's collection of odd bags and shopping carts was always parked near the Bottom Line on Fourth Street. The panhandler with a new line each time—yesterday it was "Yo, man, help me get my Mercedes out of hock"—didn't stray far from Greenwich Avenue. Everyone needs to claim a little bit of turf that belongs to him.

I was talking to Kim on the phone. "Come on over. You haven't even seen it yet."

"Yes I have."

"I mean, it's all fixed up now. I want to show you."

"I would, but I've got a French test tomorrow. A big one . . . If you want to help, you know, quiz me, I'd—

"Okay, sure. Bring your books over."

It was dinner hour, and Dad would be at Cecilia's until late. Lorraine had a rehearsal; she wouldn't be back before midnight. It was just getting dark, and there was the view of city lights from my window. I had a bunch of Temptations tapes ready to go. We'd get through her French and then . . .

Kim came in. "It's cold out there. It's beginning to feel like winter." Her cheeks were rosy and her eyes were bright.

"God, you're so beautiful!" I unwrapped the scarf from around her neck and wrapped her in a hug. She leaned against me, soft and warm.

We went up to my room arm in arm.

"It turned out awfully well," she said.

"Except I wish the wall in the middle could come down, but—"

"No, two separate areas is good." She walked around, touching things. "And there's that wonderful carving. I never imagined—everything looks great!"

I smiled back at her, trying not to look too dumbly proud.

"Really nice," she said. "You did a terrific job."

"Thanks. I wanted you to like it."

"Oh, I do!"

We had both been trying extra hard to be nice, ever since the night at the shelter. We hadn't mentioned it, but the strain of questions unasked and unanswered hung between us. I thought, tonight, alone in my room, we'd get to feeling closer.

"Well . . . should we get started on the French?" she asked.

"Yeah, let's get it over with."

She looked around. "Where do we sit?"

"On the bed."

She glanced at the expanse of black satin and raised her eyebrow.

"Kim, I don't have any chairs yet. That's the only place."

"Oh. All right."

She conjugated a slew of regular verbs and irregular verbs. I drilled her on long vocabulary lists. First, English to French. Then, French to English. She made only two little gender mistakes.

"You know this," I told her.

"Let's go over the words I missed. I have to remember, *la vérité* is feminine."

"Okay."

"*La vérité. La vérité,*" she repeated over and over.

"You know this perfectly. You've got a sure A."

She bit her lip. "Maybe I need more review. This test is half my grade."

"You've got it down backward and forward. You're making yourself crazy over nothing."

"Do you think so? I guess you're right."

"Whenever you're nervous, you chew on your lips," I said.

"I do? Oh. I didn't realize . . . I'm sorry."

I laughed. "Don't be *sorry*." I moved closer. "I was just thinking we could put them to better use."

We settled into a long, long kiss. Kim was into it, I could swear to that. I mean, you can tell when a girl is really feeling something . . .

"Wait," I mumbled. I got up and doused the lights. The city sparkled through the window. I turned on the tape deck and the Temptations filled the room.

She was sitting on the bed watching me, her legs curled under her, her lips parted; I was drawn back to her like a nail to a magnet. Kim was the one I wanted—not The Redhead, not Marisa, not Moira, not Lizabeth. Only Kim. I was never more sure of anything in my life. Another deep kiss, and there were hot shivers down to my toes.

"Remember, we said we'd have our own song?" I whispered into her hair.

"Uh-huh." I felt her breath against my neck.

"When something special is happening . . ."

We tipped back on the bed, our arms tight around each other. I felt the length of her body pressing against mine while the Temptations reached an emotional peak.

My hands wandered, and she was melting into me. I touched her, I heard her quick intake of breath, and I felt my whole body shudder—

Suddenly, she was sitting upright. "No! Cut it out! I've told you and told you!"

I don't know how she could wrench herself out of the mood so fast. I was still fuzzy. "Kim—"

"We're not doing this! We're just not!"

"Jeez!" I exhaled a stream of air. "Why not? It's the most natural—"

Her words rushed together in one long uninterrupted flow. "I'm not ready, we're too young, if you really cared about me you wouldn't pressure me—"

"If you really cared about me, you'd want to."

She jumped up. She was pacing the room. "Those girls at the shelter. Those girls with their babies. They weren't any older than me. You said they were playing Barbie dolls."

"What? What does that have to do with—"

She was coming out of left field again, really upset. "They won't be 'dolls' forever! What happens to them then? No one has the right to have kids they can't take care of. No one!"

"Kim, if that's what—I'd use something. I'm responsible. I'm not stupid. Could you please stand still? I'm trying to talk to you."

"And AIDS. What about AIDS?"

"Kim, neither one of us has been with anyone else."

"I don't want to! I'm not ready!"

I took a deep breath. "I'm not saying it has to be all the way. I never said that. I'm just saying, a little more. Everybody else . . . We've been going out for a long time and we can't just keep *kissing*. It's got to go to something more. Some infinitesimally small amount of . . . progress."

Her voice was shaking. "I won't do anything I wouldn't want my parents to know about. I want them to be proud of me. I won't—"

"How did your *parents* get into this? What are you talking about?"

She shook her head, on the verge of tears. She mystified me. I'd never understand her. Never. And I was getting tired of trying.

"I don't think this is working out," I said. "I've had it."

"Because of sex? You'd break up with me just because of sex? That really stinks!"

"No," I said. "Not just that. Everything you do. Your whole prima donna scene at the shelter; it wasn't *tidy* enough for you. You're so neat—no, *meticulous*! And my party. You even had to be a perfectionist about the damn wallpaper! The original Energizer rabbit, always bucking for grades!"

I got up and went to the bathroom. I splashed cold water over my face. When I came back to my room, all the lights were on, and Kim's hair was neatly combed. She was sitting stiffly on the bed, her French book hugged tight against her chest. The Temptations were still going strong, pathetic in the frigid atmosphere.

I sat down too, a careful twelve inches away.

I'd said too much and I wished I'd kept my big mouth shut. But, no question about it, there was a problem here. My girlfriend was incredibly uptight, and I had a body that was going haywire.

I'd read in *National Geographic* about this tribe somewhere—I forget where, South Seas or something. As soon as a boy reaches puberty, they do a manhood ritual dance and then they give him his own private hut. The girls who've reached puberty go into his hut and have sex with him. If he especially likes one girl, he can invite her to move in with him and the tribe celebrates with a big feather dance. I could do without all that dancing, but the rest makes a lot more sense than the American way. I mean, you get a full blast of hormones before you're fifteen, but you're a pig if you pressure your girlfriend and you can't get married until you're twenty-something, so what are you supposed to do in the meantime?

I know a lot of people do what they want anyway. At least Kim wasn't a hypocrite. I had to respect her for that. I glanced at her. She was looking straight ahead.

"I'm sorry," I said. "I didn't really mean that."

I was afraid she was going to cry. She always made me feel like the bad guy.

We sat for the longest time, not saying anything. I kept feeling worse and worse. The tape ran down; the only sound in the room was the faint whir of the machine. It was excruciatingly awkward.

"Kim, I really like you," I finally said. "I always did, but . . . this is either going to get better, or it has to go downhill. And I don't want to see it getting worse to where we don't even like each other at all . . ."

"I don't want to break up!" she exploded. "I won't!"

I hesitated. "We're so different and—you don't open up about anything. I never know what's going on with you. If you'd just *tell* me . . ."

Kim looked terribly distressed. I waited, but she didn't volunteer a word.

I knew she was very pretty. She knew I had a good

vocabulary. That wasn't enough. Maybe we didn't know each other at all.

I plunged on. "I guess we should think about whether this is working out."

"It's just too much right now! You're putting so much pressure on me, and with school and tests and—and those shelter kids! It's too much!"

"I'm sorry," I said. "I swear I try not to, but . . ." A little while ago, I was so sure it was only Kim for me; not The Redhead, not Marisa, et cetera, et cetera. Was that just the heat of the moment? I couldn't even trust my own head anymore.

"It's late. I have to get home," she said.

"I know." I got up. "I'll walk you."

She looked up at me. Her eyes were wet. "I don't *want* us to break up!"

I didn't know what to answer.

"I'll call you tomorrow after school," I said. "We'll get together and talk some more."

THE next morning Lorraine shook me awake before my alarm clock went off.

"Andy! I don't know what to do!"

I opened one eye. "Do about what?" I said groggily.

"Come here. You can see it from your window."

"What time is it anyway?" I staggered to my feet.

"Look!" She opened the window and pointed down.

I leaned out. A large cardboard box and unmatched sheets of plywood were arranged like a lean-to within the iron fenced area at our front door. One of the pieces of plywood was somehow rigged to our lantern.

"What's going on?" I said. "What is that?"

"There's a man in it! It's like he's just taken up residence at our house!"

I pulled on my jeans. "I'll tell him to go," I said.

"No, wait. He's a big guy. He might be drunk or crazy or—he was talking to himself. Loud."

"Well, Dad and I will—"

"Your father left for the fish market at four o'clock. He must have built it after that."

"Do you want to just leave him there?"

"No, I can't even get out of the house without bumping into it!" Lorraine was upset.

"Should we wait for Dad?"

"Lazlo's going to Cecilia's from the market, but he's probably stopped somewhere for breakfast and—I don't know where he'd be now."

"I'll go down, Lorraine, and—"

"No, don't. What if he gets violent? Do you think we should call the police?"

"That seems kind of extreme," I said. "The guy's not actually *in* our house."

"Maybe he'll go away by himself," Lorraine said hopefully.

"Maybe." But the thing he'd built looked like he had permanent plans. "Uh—let's have some breakfast first. I can't even think." My clock read 7:10. I didn't have to be up for another half hour.

We had coffee and toast at the kitchen table. Well, I did. Lorraine kept jumping up to check at the front window.

"He's still there."

"Maybe we should call the cops before I leave for school," I said.

"I guess."

"Lorraine, please sit down." She was making me nervous. "Relax and have your coffee."

"Andy, look! He's coming out of the box."

I joined her at the window. He was a huge raggedy guy with stringy blond hair. He was standing up, stretching and scratching his stomach. Then he seemed to be checking one of the plywood sheets and adjusting it. He scratched some more and walked outside of our gate.

"Looks like he's going," Lorraine said.

"Yeah, probably to get himself a welcome mat."

"Not funny."

We watched him heading down the street. He had a peculiar rolling gait.

"Let's get rid of his stuff while he's gone," I said.

"Quick, before he gets back."

We raced outside, both of us half-dressed. There were three plywood sheets. One of them had a wire attached that was twisted around the lamppost. It took forever to unwind it.

"Hurry," Lorraine was saying.

I wound up breaking it. We dragged the plywood to the curb. Inside the cardboard box was a frying pan and a torn sweatshirt. Lorraine picked it up gingerly and held it away from her. I carried the box and piled it on the wood. We put his stuff on top.

"Do you see him? Is he coming back yet?"

"No."

We shoved the pile along the curb, down the street a bit. Away from our house. And then we rushed back inside.

"Well, that's done!" Lorraine was energetically washing her hands.

"Mission accomplished," I said. "I guess he'll get the point."

"I certainly hope so."

"I have to go to school pretty soon," I said. "Unless you want me to stay?"

"No, I'll be leaving a little while after you. I've got a dance class this morning and—"

"Just be sure to lock up," I said.

"Well, of course. I always do," Lorraine said.

"He'll set up housekeeping someplace else," I said.

"So that's that," Lorraine said.

We finished breakfast. I took a long, hot shower and got dressed. When I came back downstairs, Lorraine was fussing with the geraniums on the windowsill. The morning was back to normal, and by the time I arrived at BT, the incident was far back in my mind.

I didn't think about it until I came home from school. I walked toward the house and I thought, Good, our front area was completely empty. I glanced at the curb. The pile was gone. It must have taken him a long time to collect all that material, I thought. I hoped the garbagemen hadn't hauled it off before he'd had a chance to come back and move it somewhere.

I unlocked the front door. "Anyone home?"

No answer.

I didn't actually notice anything until I was already in the house. Shards of red glass and a rock were on the floor. It took me a moment to make the connection: the red pane from the stained-glass window. Someone had heaved the rock through it. That was *my* stained-glass window in *my* house and I was overwhelmed with rage.

Katie was winding around my legs to greet me, and I quickly shooed her away. If she got a glass splinter in her paw, I would *kill*! I swept up the mess and felt the adrenaline pumping through me. I took a hammer from the kitchen drawer and went outside. I looked up and down the street. If I'd seen him at that moment, huge or not, I would have bashed him!

I examined the window. Luckily, he'd only gotten one pane. We'd never be able to match it exactly, but it could be patched somehow. God, I didn't look forward to telling Lorraine.

I went inside and there was the hammer, still in my hand. Would I have used it on him because of a *window*? I put it back in the drawer. Compassion for the homeless sure flew away fast in the face of NIMBY. Not In My Back Yard. Well, this was my own actual front stoop that had been invaded.

In a strange kind of way, I understood him. We'd wrecked his "house," so he got even on ours. But he had no right! There was such a thing as private property. *My* property. That guy sure looked able-bodied enough to work. Well, he had tried to build something for himself . . .

Nothing was black and white. I was muddling through shades of gray. And I'd been down on Kim for not being sympathetic enough. Kim—I had promised to call her right after school!

Mrs. O'Hara answered the phone. "No, she hasn't come home yet, Andy."

"Oh. Could you please tell her I called?"

"Yes, of course. She should be here by now . . . I thought she might be with you."

"No . . . She probably stopped off somewhere."

"Well, I'll tell her you called."

I wasn't sorry that I hadn't reached her. I was more than willing to postpone the talk we were supposed to have. I didn't know what I wanted. I liked Kim—but it wasn't much fun anymore. But I *liked* her. But . . .

Ambivalence, your name is Andy Szabo.

KIM didn't call me back that afternoon. She was probably mad at me. Maybe *she* wanted to break up now—and that thought made me want her all over again. Well, I wasn't about to chase after her.

It was after nine. Dad had just come from Cecilia's; Cajun Jack was handling the late shift. I was in the living room trying to read *Pride and Prejudice* for American lit. I don't know, Jane Austen doesn't do it for me.

"Lazlo, it's getting very strange," Lorraine was saying. "I can understand a director being creative, but—"

"Maybe it won't be that bad," Dad said.

"He says Shakespeare needs updating. He's setting it in the East Village. King Lear is a drug kingpin and the daughters are streetwalkers."

I looked up from my book. "They are?"

"Well, me—Goneril—and Regan. Cordelia, the good daughter, is an environmental activist."

The phone rang. I went to answer it. It was Mr. O'Hara.

"Andy, is Kim with you?"

"Kim? No."

"Have you heard from her?" I caught the strain in his voice.

"No, I left a message before, but—she didn't come home yet?"

"Maybe she's having dinner at a friend's house but . . . It's not like her not to let us know," Mr. O'Hara said. There was an uncomfortable pause. "Tracey forgets sometimes, but not Kim."

No, not Kim, I thought.

"It's not that late, but . . . Did she say anything to you last night? About having plans for this afternoon?"

"No, nothing," I said. A beat of silence. "She'll probably show up any minute," I added.

"I'm sure she will. Sorry to bother you. Thanks, Andy."

I went back to Jane Austen. I couldn't concentrate. The expression on Kim's face the night before . . . I'd made her miserable. I had no business hassling her like that. It was wrong, dead wrong.

"Kim is missing!" I blurted.

"She's what?" Dad said. "Since when?"

"She never came home from school. She's not home yet."

"I wouldn't worry, it's only nine-thirty," Lorraine said. "Andy, there've been lots of times when you didn't come home until later."

I know," I said, "but I'm different. You could set a clock by Kim O'Hara."

I tried to get through another page of Jane Austen and then I slammed the book shut.

"I'm going over there," I said.

Mr. O'Hara looked haggard. Mrs. O'Hara was pale; her freckles stood out. Even Tracey was subdued.

'Was she in school today?" I asked.

"Yes," Mr. O'Hara said. Her pink address book was in his hand. "We've been calling . . . Bettina Lord saw her in homeroom. Karen Garcia was in social studies with her in the morning; she said Kim was quiet, didn't raise her hand at all—but then, Kim gets those quiet moods sometimes. . . ."

"We're not sure who's from Science," Mrs. O'Hara said, "or who's from camp and—"

"Maybe there's someone I know," I said. "Someone I could call."

Mr. O'Hara handed the book to me. I riffled through the pages. Her precise, neat handwriting stabbed at me. Under *S*, I saw my name, circled by little hearts.

"Laurie Thompson," I said. "I met her once. She lives on Twenty-third Street; Kim takes the subway downtown with her."

"Please," Mrs. O'Hara said, "talk to her." Her voice sounded choked.

I dialed the number. "Could I please speak to Laurie?"

"I think she might be in the shower . . . just a minute . . . Who is this?"

"Andy Szabo."

"Andy what?"

"*S-Z-A*—I'm a friend of Kim O'Hara. Kim O'Hara, from Science. It's important."

"Well, just a minute, please."

"Tell her it's very important."

I waited. The O'Haras stared at me numbly. Tracey was nervously twirling her hair.

"Hello?"

"Laurie? This is Andy Szabo. I met you at Dominic's Pizzeria once, I was with Kim O'Hara—"

"Oh sure, Kim's boyfriend."

"Yes," I said. "The thing is, Kim never came home

from school today, and her folks are worried. Do you know if she was going anyplace or?—"

"She left school early. Right after French."

"She did? Did something happen?"

"Well, yes. Didn't she go home?"

"No." I was filled with dread. "What happened?"

"Gosh, I hope she's all right."

"What happened?"

The O'Haras were listening to me intently. Mrs. O'Hara clutched her husband's hand.

"We had a big French test today. I sit two seats from Kim, and I looked over at her. She wasn't writing anything. She was just staring at the test paper. It was like she froze."

"I studied with her last night," I said. "She knew everything."

"I know, she's awfully good in French. Well, she didn't write a thing on the page. And halfway through, she just got up and left the test on her desk and ran out of the room. I thought maybe she was sick and went straight home, because I didn't see her in physics later and—she wasn't at the front steps after school either; that's where I meet her to go home."

"Oh."

"She's okay, isn't she?" Laurie said.

"I don't know."

I repeated the conversation to the O'Haras.

"I'm calling the police!" Mr. O'Hara said. "Right now!" He dialed, and Tracey began to whimper.

"My daughter is missing! . . . Kim. Kim O'Hara. She's only fifteen and—twenty-three Fifth Avenue. Five five five, three four two oh . . . Since today. She was in school this morning, but she left early and she never came home . . . No. She wouldn't do that. . . . No, you don't understand. . . . No, she's completely reliable, she's an ideal student and—my daughter is *missing*!"

Mr. O'Hara left the telephone, defeated, clenching and unclenching his fists. "She hasn't been gone long enough for a missing persons report. They said—they said kids cut school, maybe she went to the movies . . . Andy, you were with her last night. Did you notice anything? Did she seem bothered by anything?"

"I—I don't think so." What else could I say? Mr. O'Hara, I tried to push your daughter into going further than she wanted. I trapped her between that and breaking up.

"It's almost eleven!" Mrs. O'Hara's voice was pitched high, like a scream. "We have to do *something*!"

Mr. O'Hara was struggling into his jacket. "I'm going out to look for her."

Mrs. O'Hara clutched his arm. "I'll go with you."

"No, no, stay here. In case someone—call the hospitals. Call the emergency rooms."

I followed Mr. O'Hara outside. "How can I help? What can I do?"

"I'll take the subway, retrace her way to school. You could check around the neighborhood. Any hangouts or—"

Kim didn't *have* any hangouts. I walked down the street, hoping against hope to see her. I covered Washington Square Park. It was a different world at night. The baby carriages, soccer players, and NYU students were gone. Benches were occupied by people sleeping under newspapers. Small clusters of people stood in the dark, making deals. Why was I looking in the *park*? It made no sense.

I walked along brightly lit streets. I looked into restaurants and piano bars and glassed-in cafes. I walked through quiet, crooked streets. Sixth Avenue, Christopher, Grove, Bedford, Greenwich. I passed the Waverly as it was emptying out. I stopped and checked all the people. I thought of that first night, the Marx Brothers movie, and I wished I could start from there and do it right this time. People were talking and laughing as they came out. How could everything seem so normal when Kim was missing?

I walked in useless circles. As long as I kept moving, in action; as long as I was doing something, not thinking . . .

When I came home, Dad and Lorraine were asleep upstairs. I called the O'Haras; I knew I wouldn't be waking anyone in that household.

"Hello?" I could hear the hope and fear mingled in Mrs. O'Hara's one word.

"It's only me. Andy. Have you heard anything?"

"No. Nothing."

"I'm home now. Would you let me know as soon as you hear? Anything at all, any time of the night."

"Yes. We will."

"Mrs. O'Hara? Kim is all right. I know she is." She has to be!

"Thank you, Andy," she said softly.

I sat down in the dining room, my head slumped on the table. I waited for the phone to ring. I prayed for good news. It was my fault. Kim was sensitive. I should have known she couldn't take any more pressure, about anything. It was my fault. And Kim was out there somewhere.

I didn't think I would, but I must have fallen asleep.
Lorraine found me in the dining room.

"Andy?"

I bolted upright in the chair. My eyes felt sandy,
and my legs and shoulders were stiff.

"Aren't you awfully late for school?"

The sunlight streaming from the window made
me squint. "I'm not going in today. Kim is still
missing."

"Are you sure? Maybe she just stayed at a friend's
house."

"No, she would have called."

My mouth tasted terrible. I staggered upstairs and
brushed my teeth. I was rinsing, with the faucet running, when I thought I heard the phone ring. I jumped
for it.

"Hello. Is Andy Szabo there?" An unfamiliar voice.

"I'm Andy."

"Oh, hello. This is Mrs. Cannon."

Who? It didn't register.

"Mrs. Cannon, from the shelter."

"Oh." I'd hoped—disappointment felt like a rock in my stomach. "Hello, Mrs. Cannon."

"This is kind of a long shot, but I thought I'd try you."

"What about?"

"When I came to work this morning, there was a girl here. Seems she came in during the night. We're not supposed to take runaways, but they let her stay in the rec room for the night."

I was holding my breath.

"She won't give anyone her name or address. Well, when I came in this morning, I thought she looked familiar. This may be a very long shot, but she looks something like that girl you brought in once. A couple of weeks ago? Of course, I just had a quick look at her, but—"

"I'll be right down!" I said. "I'll be right there!"

I ran down the stairs and I thought, Kim? In the *shelter*? It couldn't be. I was going to call the O'Haras, and then I thought I couldn't put them through that; it might not be Kim at all.

*   *   *

The rec room was full. There were people crowded on the lone couch. The television set was blaring. For a moment I was disoriented; it looked different when it was used for the kids.

She was huddled by herself in a far corner. She was sitting on the floor, curled small, her arms hugging her body. Her face was dirty; as I came closer, I could see the lines tears had made. I'd never seen her look so messy.

She didn't notice me approach. She was staring into nothing.

"Kim?"

She started.

"Kim? Why? What are you doing here?"

"This is where I belong." She gulped air between words. "This is exactly where I belong."

She held her shoulders stiff and cramped.

I squatted on the floor next to her. "Kim, everyone's been so worried. I didn't know where to look for you and—What happened?"

"I—I rode the subways for a long time. And then I walked. I was so tired and—it was dark and—"

She looked all alone and lost. I wanted to hold her, but I didn't dare to yet. "Kim, I'm sorry. I'm sorry, I—"

"I failed," she whispered.

French? Was that what this was about?

"All because of a *test*?" I tried to put my arms around her shoulders, but she curled them forward, curled them in upon herself. "It doesn't matter. Your folks know about it; they don't care."

She shook her head.

"Kim?" I touched her arm. It was icy.

"I'm not Kimberly O'Hara," she said.

I stared at her, shocked. An awful crawling feeling started at the base of my spine. "Of course you're—"

"I'm not Kimberly O'Hara. I did something terrible."

"Nothing is *that* bad," I said. "Everyone gets in trouble sometime and—" I was stunned. I didn't know how to handle this. My heart was hammering; we needed help. I spoke as gently as I could. "Come on, you're Kim and I'm—"

"I don't know what to do." Her breath sounded ragged. "I have to tell someone. Can I trust you?"

"Yes, of course."

"Promise you'll never say anything. To anyone, ever. Promise me." Her eyes locked into mine.

"I promise."

"Promise, no matter what."

"I swear, no matter what." I was scared. I didn't know what I was promising.

"My name is Tuyet."

"Come on, Kim—"

"My name is Tuyet and my brother's name is Phuong. I don't know a last name."

"No, Kim. No. You don't have a brother." I looked around frantically for Mrs. Cannon. Someone, anyone! Had she gone *crazy*? "Your sister's Tracey, they're waiting for you at home and—" I needed help!

"It's not my home. I don't have a home."

Her mind couldn't have snapped that fast, could it? Could it? "Your mom and dad are waiting and—"

"Our mother was a bar girl when all the soldiers were still in Saigon. It must have been Saigon. It was a big city." Her voice sounded dead.

"Hey, Kim, come on. Please." What was I supposed to do? I didn't know what to do!

"Our fathers were Americans; anyone could tell by the way we looked. When the Americans went away, the bar business wasn't good, and she worked the streets. But there wasn't enough money anymore or food, and one day she left us. I don't know how old I was; I don't know when I was born."

If she was hallucinating, I should call the O'Haras! Where was Mrs. Cannon? An adult or . . . I was afraid to leave her for even a minute. I kept absolutely still, afraid to move.

"I was very small and Phuong was bigger. We were on the street and he took care of me. It was hard; he was only a boy and we were *bui-doi*. That means the dust of life. Dust in the street, blown away by any wind. *Bui-doi*, half-Americans, from foreign soldiers and good-time girls. I was always hungry. Phuong went every day to find food for us. All I can remember about my mother is long, dark hair; but I remember Phuong. I can see his face."

She stopped and closed her eyes. I was paralyzed. I couldn't say a word. Across the room, a beer commercial blared from the TV. There were people talking, loud, and little kids wriggling on the floor. Someone sang out a line from a song. No one I could go to.

Her eyes opened and she looked at me from far away.

"I got a cut on my leg. It must have been infected because my leg became swollen. Double-size. Phuong was scared; he didn't know how to make it better. We walked and walked. It hurt so much. Some of the time he carried me. Phuong found the orphanage and begged Sister Thanh to take us in. It was too crowded. There were orphans everywhere. Because of the war."

Where was this nightmare coming from? I didn't know what to do!

"There wasn't enough food, not enough of anything. The medicine ran out. I slept on a mat with Mai and Chao. Mai coughed all the time, and one morning her body was cold. I woke up and touched her hand and it was cold. But it was better than the streets. Sister Thanh made my leg heal. We stayed."

She ran her hands through her hair. I watched her, hypnotized and afraid of what was coming next.

"Dad—Mr. O'Hara—was looking for his little girl. After her mother died, she'd lived with her grandparents in a village in the Mekong Delta. In the country, where the rice paddies used to be. He went there, but the grandparents were gone. Maybe they had trouble because their daughter had worked for the Americans. She was an interpreter, you know."

"I know," I said hoarsely. "You told me." This part was true. . . .

"I did? Oh."

The people across the room were loud. They were arguing about switching channels. I had to strain to hear Kim.

"He went to orphanages, looking. When he came to ours, Phuong hid and listened to the American

165

talking to Sister Thanh. He talked part Vietnamese and part English, but Phuong understood some of it." She sighed and passed her hand over her forehead. "The man said he knew her name—Kimberly, that's an unusual name in Vietnam, and she'd be five now, and she'd lived in the Mekong Delta."

This was *real*! Kim hadn't lost touch with reality. I felt relieved, so relieved that she wasn't out of her mind; and then what she was saying to me registered. I stared at her, chilled and numb all at the same time.

"Phuong found me. He was excited; he said I was the right size and this was my chance. He said to run to the American and take his hand. To tell Sister Thanh that he looked just like the photograph in my grandmama's house, in the country where the rice paddies used to be. To tell that my name used to be Kimly. To say that Phuong wasn't my real brother; he'd only helped me in the streets. I was afraid. Phuong said he would beat me if I didn't. I couldn't remember all of it. Phuong made me repeat it over and over. He said if I did it, I would go to a place with more food than I could eat and a bed all to myself. I was afraid, but I always obeyed Phuong. He pinched my arm hard, he pushed me and said, 'Go! Do it now! Hurry, before the tall American leaves!' So I went to the room where Sister Thanh was drinking tea with Mr. O'Hara. I took his hand, like Phuong said. They asked questions and I was trembling, but I said what Phuong told me, or I said, 'I don't remember.' Sister Thanh started to repeat it to the tall American in English. But he had heard me say 'Kimly,' and he picked me up and hugged me tight. I was so scared of him.

"Dad always says he knew it was me right away because I had my Grandma O'Hara's cute nose and my mother's smile. He says I get my brains from my mother. He says he'll never forget the moment I took his hand; he didn't know whether to laugh or cry, so he did both. When I took his hand, he knew it was me right away."

I reached for Kim's hand. It was limp.

"Now you know. I did this. I stole her family from Kimberly O'Hara. I tried to be good. I tried."

She hugged herself and, doubled over, began to rock.

"Does—does something hurt?" I asked.

"Yes," she whispered. Then, "I tried so hard. But I'm too tired. I can't do it anymore. I'm only Tuyet from a soldier and a good-time girl. I'm so tired. This is where I belong. *Bui-doi.*"

"Hey, don't. Don't say that." I didn't know how

to talk to her. It was too much for me to take in. "You have a home. Your mom and dad—I mean—you know they love you."

"They wouldn't if they knew."

"Come on, Kim." I raised her to her feet and she didn't resist. "I'm getting you out of here. I have to tell your folks I found you, and then I'm taking you home."

She let me lead her down the hall. She was limp, a sleepwalker. There was a graffiti-scarred pay phone. I held her close and groped for a quarter. She stood still, passive, while I called the O'Haras. Their happy relief didn't make me feel any better.

Kim let me take her outside. In the daylight, her lips looked bloodless. There were hollows under her eyes. I put my arm around her tight, and I felt her shivering. I steered her through the streets, grimy in the pale sunlight. Houston Street, I thought; there'd be cabs on Houston. I didn't say anything. I held her close.

Finally, a cab stopped for us. I helped her into it.

I sat rigid on the leather upholstery. Tuyet, Phuong, Sister Thanh. The unfamiliar names raced through my mind. I couldn't think. My eyes felt gritty. The cab swerved through traffic. In the distance, a police siren screamed.

I searched for something comforting to tell her.

"You need to get some sleep. Everything will look better when you've had some sleep."

"No. It won't." Her face contorted. "I never saw him again. He was only a little boy. I don't know where . . . " She sagged against the seat, exhausted. "I've lost Phuong."

I left Kim in the arms of her family that morning. I didn't stay. I didn't know how she would explain her breakdown, if that's what it was. I didn't want to be there.

I was reeling. Kim. Tuyet. I had never really known her at all. Now I knew too much. That gave me a responsibility, and I didn't know what to do with it.

I went home, showered, and picked up my books. I went to school, on automatic pilot. I'd missed most of my morning classes, but I didn't especially care. I couldn't stop thinking about Kim. She was amazing to have pulled it off for so long. And then I thought, Her mother was a *prostitute*; that had to be terrible for Kim to know. I wished I hadn't tried to make out with her all the time. She went around and around in my mind.

There was a phone booth near the main door. I wanted to check if she was all right. What if she had blurted everything out? I couldn't call. I couldn't talk to the O'Haras right now. Or Kim.

I loitered in the first floor hall in front of the school psychologist's office. I guess I was desperate enough to wonder if Dr. Dindonner could give me some answers.

Right, we were supposed to call him Howie. He tried hard to be open, one of the kids. He made an effort to sprinkle his conversation with choice phrases like "Oh, wow, man" and "groovy!" I guess that's why hardly anyone ever went in to see him.

I didn't know what to do. I needed help to know how to help Kim.

His office door was wide open and he was sitting at his desk, staring out into the hall. I hesitated in the doorway. When he saw me, he jumped to his feet.

"What's dragging you down?" he said, beaming.

No, I thought, not Dr. D.

"Let it all hang out, man," he said. "Let your hair hang down."

"No thanks," I said. I started down the hall.

"Andy," he called after me, "if you have a prob-lem—"

"No. Everything's cool." I got away from him fast.

Some of the kids passing by gave me strange looks.

I didn't know what I'd been thinking of. Dr. Dindonner wouldn't have the magic solution, for sure.

What could I do? Persuade her to tell her father the truth, at which point they'd all embrace and live happily ever after? But what if they didn't?

I wasn't that persuasive; Kim would never tell.

Talk to her father myself? If it went wrong, it would be all my fault. Anyway, I could never say anything; I had promised.

How long could Kim hold on? What if she blanked out on another test?

It wasn't my responsibility.

Kim *was* my responsibility.

I felt like I was juggling a hot potato. I didn't *want* Kim's problems to be on my shoulders anymore. And that made me feel like a sniveling, low-down, rock-bottom rat.

BT's lunchroom is small, too small to permit cliques. Mostly, the whole tenth grade sits at two long tables. I started to carry my tray over to my friends, but halfway there, I knew I was in no mood for the chatter and laughs. I saw a small empty table at the side and sat down alone.

I was just beginning to examine the mysterious mass of steaming brown pellets on my plate—BT believes in health food—when The Redhead bounced over.

"Okay if I sit down or are you being exclusive?"

"It's all right, Prudence Jane. Sit down."

"Can't handle Moira's narrative today?"

"Not if it's a *long* story."

We grinned at each other and started attacking our food. The Redhead was unusually quiet.

Then, "Andy, I know something's wrong. . . . Do you feel like talking?"

"What do you mean?"

"The whole school knows about Howie chasing you down the hall. I figured if you were going to see *Howie*, of all people, you must have really flipped."

"It's about someone else's problem. I can't tell you."

"Oh. Okay."

"I can't tell anyone." I turned something over with my fork. "What is this?"

"Mung beans."

"Mung? Sounds like a disease. I've got a bad case of the Mung."

"Sexually transmitted, no doubt," The Redhead said.

"I wish."

We ate in silence for a while.

"Tell me something," I said. "Do you really see a shrink for assertiveness training?"

She laughed. "No. That's just an excuse for when I want to say something outrageous."

"But do you see a shrink at all?"

"Yes."

"Why?" I asked.

"That's kind of personal," she said.

"Right. Sorry, dumb question." I was embarrassed.

"My parents split a year ago, and I had trouble handling it. Logically, I know it wasn't my fault, but I still have a lot of guilt."

"Is he helping you?"

"Yes, a lot."

I never would have thought The Redhead had a serious side. She was surprising me.

"I'd recommend him," she continued. "Dr. Alan Selig, right here in the Village. A psychologist, not a psychiatrist. He's a real person, Andy. Nothing like Howie."

"Does he tell you what to do? Like, if you're in a bind, can he come up with a solution?"

"Not really. He helps me sort out my feelings. I'm learning to deal with things."

I thought about it for a minute. "Would you write down his name and number?"

"Sure." She tore a page out of her loose-leaf and scribbled on it. "Whatever it is, if you ever feel like talking . . . Your friend Prudence Jane can be a good listener."

"Thanks," I said. I folded the page and put it in my pocket. "I would, but . . . I can't. Not about this."

I knew I had to go to see Kim that evening, no matter how uncomfortable it felt. I didn't know what I would say, but I had to go over there.

On the way, I passed the all-night Korean deli on Sixth Avenue. There were cut flowers out in front; they were shriveling in the cold. On impulse, I took a bunch of white chrysanthemums from a large container. In my hand, they looked too skimpy. I bought another bunch. They still didn't look that great, but there wasn't much of a choice.

Outside Kim's building I saw some little kids painted with garish makeup. Huge scarlet lips; they looked grotesque. For a second I thought I'd conjured them out of a disturbed mind. No—how could I have forgotten?—it was Halloween.

Mr. O'Hara let me in.

I stopped in the entry. "How is she?" I asked

carefully. I could hear scales being mechanically pounded out on the piano.

"She's fine," he said. "It was just one of those things, taking a test too seriously. She's such a good student—she's so used to doing well that she overreacted, that's all."

"Oh."

"Blanking out on a test," he said. "That happens."

Kim turned from the piano when I entered the living room. "Hello." She looked fresh and scrubbed, back to normal. I don't know what I'd expected.

"Hi." I held out the bouquet awkwardly.

"Thank you." She studied me; this was the cool, collected Kim. "You never gave me flowers before."

"No. I guess I should have."

"I'll put them in water."

I followed her into the kitchen. I watched her fill the vase and trim the stems. She got busy, arranging and rearranging the mums.

"You look like you're feeling better," I finally said.

"I slept all day," she said.

"So you're right back to the piano practice."

"Yes, why not? I'm fine."

"I thought—"

"What? That I'd be an invalid?" she said. "Is that why you brought flowers?"

"No. I just wanted to."

"Why?"

"Why did I *want* to? Because I—" I didn't know what to say.

She watched me, waiting.

Some of the petals were already dropping.

"You're going to be so careful with me now, aren't you?" she said. "You'll be so afraid to break up with me now."

"Kim, I—"

"And it's going to be awful."

"Maybe I am tiptoeing a little," I admitted. "After last night—"

"I don't want to see you anymore," she said.

I was stunned. "Why? What did I do?" A beat. "Kim, I'm sorry about the other night. I was wrong. I don't know what was the matter with me."

"Because you saw me falling apart. Well, that won't happen again."

"Look, there are a lot of things I understand now."

"Forget about it. I never told you anything. It never happened."

"No, I won't forget about it."

"Go away, Andy. Go home."

"I'm not leaving. Not until we talk about Tuyet."

"Not in this house," she hissed. "Not here."

We walked along Fifth Avenue. Traffic was jammed in some kind of gridlock. Car horns honked in a frenzy.

"Because of the parade," I said.

Kim nodded. "It gets bigger every year."

"It was better when it was mostly Village people. It got too popular."

Car exhausts were spewing fumes. We turned west at Waverly Place. It was past twilight; it was getting dark earlier.

"I don't have a costume this year," I said. "I forgot about it. There's a party at Garrity's later . . ."

A pack of Hell's Angels lurched by us. Couldn't tell if they were the real thing or a bunch of accountants from New Jersey. Whichever, they'd had an early start on the night's drinking.

"I always tried to be scary," Kim said. "A witch or a devil."

I smiled. "Completely out of character."

"No," she said. "Evil isn't that much of a stretch."

"Kim, don't. Given the time and place, you did the best you could. You can't keep beating yourself up."

She shrugged.

"It's too much for you to carry all by yourself."

"No, I'll go on just like always. I'm fine."

"You've got to *do* something."

"What do you expect me to do? 'Good morning, Dad. By the way, I'm not your daughter. She was left behind someplace.'"

"He told you himself, it was like looking for a needle in a haystack. He might never have found her. She could have died or—"

"Or he might have. It's her home, not mine. Nothing really belongs to me."

A ragged man shook his cup at us. "Trick or treat." He grinned. There was a black hole where his front tooth should have been.

"I honestly don't know if you should tell them, but—"

"I won't! Not ever!"

"—but you've got to talk to somebody. Maybe your priest or—"

She shook her head. "I haven't gone to confession in years. I used to make up *little* sins."

"Listen, a friend of mine—" I almost said The Redhead, but I caught myself; I remembered Kim didn't like her. "A friend of mine sees a psychologist. Dr. Alan Selig. He's right here in the Village and she says he's really good. Kim, you need to talk to some-body."

"No, I don't."

"I'm not good enough. I don't know anything; I don't know what to tell you." I took the piece of loose-leaf out of my pocket. "Here. His name and number. Come on, take it."

She hesitated.

"Just take it, all right?"

She put it in her purse without looking at it.

We walked past a row of town houses. Lights were on in most of them. I caught glimpses of a bookcase, a chandelier, a bright red wall. A jack-o'-lantern winked from a window. I wondered about the people who lived there. It looked so inviting from the outside.

"You can go on home," she said. "You're off the hook."

"What does that mean?"

"You don't have do anything else. You wanted to break up before, so—nothing's any different."

"Everything's different. I'm just beginning to know you; I don't want to walk away."

"You don't want to be my boyfriend either. . . . I'm still not going to have sex with you."

"That's okay. I was thinking, you were right. It would have been too heavy; we weren't ready for . . . Maybe I shouldn't be your *boyfriend* right now, but—"

She nodded. "I know. So—you can take off. Go to your party or—"

"Stop sending me away. There's got to be something between boyfriend and exile."

She stopped walking and faced me. "What *do* you want?" She sounded exasperated.

"I don't know. I don't know exactly how to say it."

A family passed by us, dressed in costume; a little Batman and a small clown running in excited circles.

"This boyfriend-girlfriend thing. It's like a lot of expectations build up," I said. "What you're supposed to do, what your friends say they're doing, the way it is on TV or—do you know what I mean?"

"Sort of," she said.

"I liked you in ninth grade, before we'd even said a word to each other, because you were so pretty. It's like I imagined whatever way I wanted you to be." I glanced at her; it was easy to project almost anything onto that unexpressive, controlled, beautiful face. "You made up some kind of image for me too. I'm not your hero, Kim. Hey, I loved having you think romantic things about me, but—"

"I still don't know what you want."

"I'm saying, getting all tied up before we really know each other is . . . it's going through the motions without any—without anything behind it." I felt like I was stumbling all over the place. "We could start off as friends and see what happens. See if we want it to be more. I'd be a better friend than a boyfriend right now."

"Are you trying to let me down easy? Don't worry, I'm not going to flip out."

"I'm not letting you down! I'm talking about being a *real friend*, and that ain't chopped liver! Unless you're just not interested. . . . I mean, you've been telling me to get lost all night."

She didn't answer for a long time. Maybe she was sick of me. Maybe she was angry about the way I'd pressured her; she had a right.

"I was embarrassed," she finally said. "After the way you saw me . . . I couldn't face you. . . . You must think I'm so weak."

"*Weak?* No way! The way you've toughed it out—I don't know that anyone else could do that. You're a survivor, Kim. You're amazing. Jeez, don't be *embarrassed* with me. I think you're terrific."

"There's nothing terrific. What I did was terrible. My whole life is a lie. I can't get out of it, but I know it's wrong."

"If you want to talk about wrong: The war was wrong. Soldiers leaving babies behind was wrong.

Children living on the streets was wrong. Who's to judge you?"

We continued walking. I took her hand and she didn't pull it away. The farther west we went, the more crowded it became. You could feel a weird kind of excitement building. Masks popping out of the dark—the Joker, Satan, an elephant face complete with tusks. Someone on stilts, high above the crowd. People jammed the sidewalks from the building line to the curb.

The parade had begun. I held tight to Kim's arm; I worried that we'd get separated. We strained to see over all the people in front of us. Feathers and sequins. Cars and floats and hands waving. A trumpet player in a gold lamé suit. Towering, elaborate constructions. Costumed kids teetering on their fathers' shoulders.

I caught the glint of Kim's smile—"Andy, look at that!"—as a lit-up Eiffel Tower marched by.

Men in lavish ball gowns and inch-long eyelashes, more funny than grotesque. Madonna and Mae West, with exaggerated bows to the crowd. Little Orphan Annie, six feet tall, strutted by with Daddy Warbucks. Almost-bare bodies covered with glitter. Ronald Reagan held up a sign that made the people in front laugh; I couldn't read it.

People and more people crowded to see. We were

jostled and elbowed. Gangs of kids, feeling no pain, yelled to each other. A lot of partying had already started. Music from the parade fought with music from a boom box in our ears. Two guys shoved past us; I held on to Kim.

She was speaking; I had to bend close to hear. "I'm getting trampled," she said.

"Me too. Let's get out of here." I put both arms around her and we fought our way through the crowd. Even the streets off the parade route were full of revelers. We ducked into a quiet cobblestoned court- yard. We stood at the edge of an iron gate, under bare branches.

"Too much craziness out there," I said.

"I should be getting home," she said. "They're awfully nervous about me now. If I'm the least bit late—"

I nodded.

"I'm perfectly fine, but they—"

"Stop telling me you're fine. You can't keep on the way you've been going. Something's gonna give."

"No. No, I'm really—"

"Kim, listen to me." I grasped her shoulders and made her face me. "No more pretend."

We stared at each other. Lantern light threw shad- ows across her face. There wasn't a sound. We might have time-tripped into another century.

She was biting her lip. "I have to go home."

"I know." I didn't know what else I could say. I released her. "I'll go with you."

She took a step away and then she turned back to me. "Andy?"

"Yes?"

"About Dr. What's-his-name—"

"Selig."

"I've—I've never been to a . . . psychologist. . . . Would you go with me? You don't have to come in or anything, but—would you just go with me? I know it's stupid, but I'm—"

"I'll go with you. I'll come in or wait outside or—whatever you want."

"Thanks. Thank you."

"That's what friends are for," I said.

She half smiled. "Okay, friend."

I hugged her. Her hair brushed against my cheek, and I smelled the familiar gardenia perfume. I was going to say, I can't swear that I'll always be strictly brotherly. . . . But I caught myself in time. She'd had a brother once.

So I was quiet and kept my arms wrapped around her.

Erika Tamar lives in New York City and the Greenwich Village setting of *The Truth about Kim O'Hara* is one of her favorite neighborhoods. She started writing about Andy Szabo in *It Happened at Cecilia's* and had so much fun with him that she couldn't resist continuing the story. Her other published young adult novels are *Blues for Silk Garcia*; *Goodbye, Glamour Girl*; *High Cheekbones* and *Out of Control*.

Ms. Tamar has three children, Ray, Monica, and Michael.